THE FIRST TIME

PAWAS JAIN

Leadstart
INKSTATE

ISBN 978-93-90463-92-3

First published in India 2020 by Inkstate Books
An imprint of Leadstart Publishing Pvt Ltd

Sales Office:
Unit No.25/26, Building No.A/1,
Near Wadala RTO,
Wadala (East), Mumbai – 400037 India
Phone: +91 969933000
Email: info@leadstartcorp.com
www.leadstartcorp.com

Disclaimer: The views expressed in this book are those of the Author and do not pertain to be held by the Publisher.

Editor: Cora Bhatia
Cover: Jitendra Mahadik
Layouts: Victor Patali

"Dedicated to my wife (still my girlfriend) Bhagyashree, for pushing me to complete this story. Without her, this book would not have been in your hands"

Twenty-eight-year-old Chartered Accountant from Jaipur, Rajasthan, Pawas Jain is the Founder and CEO of **The TBC Group**, which owns multiple business verticals, the prominent face being **TBC Consulting**, one of India's fastest growing Marketing Consulting companies.

He co-founded one of the first funded startups of Rajasthan, **Blue Box Media Pvt. Ltd.**, backed by Angel funds in 2013.

Pawas Jain has been a pioneer in the Digital Content space in India, and started his first content venture in 2010 with **SpringTide**, which gained mass following over the years.

Now, **TBC Consulting** works with leading brands and startups across the country on brand building, marketing and content production. TBC Consulting has consulted over 75 brands over a period of 4 years on marketing and content, including the likes of Arttd'inox, UClean Group, Revv, Jawa Motorcycles, Smart Kidz Club and many others. It was awarded as one of the **Top 20 Startup Consultancy Companies of 2018 by Silicon India Magazine,** and has recently expanded its footprints in London starting March 2020.

The company owns multiple other business verticals such as **TechSamvad, LivUp, FireFly, Indian Chai Company**, across different domains and sectors.

Pawas currently mentors over 15 startups in VR / AR, Education, Finance and Media domains. He is a professionally trained Visharad in tabla.

You can reach him at <u>pawas@thetbcgroup.com</u> or Connect with him on LinkedIn at <u>https://www.linkedin.com/in/ pawasjain/</u>

This book is a dream—a dream I envisioned 15 years ago, at a very young age—of becoming a published author, one day. My distant dream every time I attended a Literature Festival or launch event was the thought—that I would be on the other side of the stage someday. I achieved many things, failed at some—worked with hundreds of businesses and entrepreneurs—watching their stories very closely. The only thing that remained constant—was the dream of being a published author.

However, saying that this book is completely mine would be unfair—unfair to those people who have been a part of this process knowingly or unknowingly, unfair to those stories that inspired me to write this tell-all insider tale of the ecosystem. At the outset, clichéd as it may sound, this book belongs to my parents—who never let my dreams die and fuelled them at every step of life. They stood behind me rock solid, during my worst phases.

This book belongs to my sister and her husband, Faguni and Adarsh, who gave me a perspective that no one else could. The honest critics of this book and people, who told me that I should push myself, take more risk and always stick to entrepreneurship—even during the hardest times when I wanted to give up.

This book also belongs to the love of my life, now my wife, Bhagyashree, who motivated me to overcome writers' block and complete the book. It takes a lot to cope up with the eccentricities and whims of an entrepreneur, a writer, and she does all of it amazingly.

This book, in the truest sense, also belongs to team members and colleagues, in my company—The TBC Group, who have worked hardest to make the company what it is today; people who have stuck with the company, worked like family, and helped it to sail through difficult times.

This book is for all those clients, associates, and people who have defined relationships and trusted me in everything I have done. People, who have appreciated, supported and stood by me in all my endeavours. People, whose stories have inspired me, unfortunately, it would be very difficult to list all of them.

This book is for those hundreds and thousands of first generation entrepreneurs in India, who dare to take a path less travelled and create genuine businesses without any support. I know the challenges and sacrifices that it takes to tread that path.

Finally and importantly, this book belongs to those who pulled me down, mocked my ways and created roadblocks. I did not succumb to the pressures, but I sincerely thank them for toughening me to face more difficult challenges in life.

Cheers to the hope that lives in each one of us and to those million dreams that get broken every day.

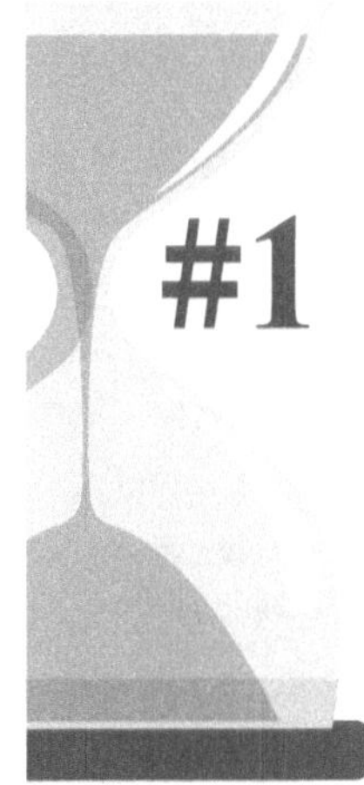

#1

'Indira Gandhi International Airport,' the signboard was visible from a distance. As the cab took a sharp left and sped beneath the direction board proclaiming 'Departures,' Raghav felt his heart throbbing in the passenger seat. He frantically checked his watch. It was 10.30 pm. He was in time.

The cab drove into the driveway for Terminal 3 and he swiftly got out of the cab with his laptop bag; the only piece of luggage he was carrying. He walked towards the entry gate, pulling out his identity proof. Ironically, identity was the only thing that had been a crisis for him in the past few years. And here he was – at the airport in the capital city of India, seven hours earlier than his flight's departure.

On entering the airport, he quickly realised that his crisis was visible on his countenance and he changed his demeanour. Now he walked more confidently as if in a place he knew too well, adjusted his specs, and looked around sharper. He held his laptop bag in one hand and phone in the other, for a seamless coordination through the new bane of the world – WhatsApp.

"I am right before the security check" – read the WhatsApp message. Raghav impatiently retrieved his boarding pass and walked towards security check, hoping that his demeanour was not betraying the sinking feeling in his heart. He could feel it beating in his stomach!

There she was—her hair flowing beautifully past her waist, the vibrant twinkle in those eyes, the smile that could change the fate of the world and the persona that exuded confidence—Riya. She saw him too and walked towards him hand outstretched at what seemed a potential handshake. Raghav, already floored watching her from a distance, approached her. His heart skipped a beat, and he pushed forward into something that seemed to be like a hug, oblivious of her outstretched hand.

"Ahan! So you are not into handshakes, it seems!" Riya beamed.

Unsure of whether this was a taunt or an appreciation, Raghav just smiled like an idiot. There were very few occasions in his life where he was short of words. This was one of them.

Comeback. Wisecrack. Stupid joke. His mind jumped from one thought to another like a wild rabbit, and he could not come up with anything. He sighed, realising that all his content creation skills had failed him.

Riya kept talking as they walked towards the centrally located Starbucks inside the airport. Raghav, lost in thought, just managed to match her pace of talking and walking. He thought about the huge turmoil that he faced last night in his company. He had decided not to take this flight to Jaipur, but he could not have missed meeting Riya. He did not tell her that he was not travelling and in fact was going back to his office, as soon as she boarded the flight.

As they took their seats at Starbucks, Riya looked at him smiling and said, "Such a happy coincidence, that you were travelling back to your hometown the same day. Otherwise, who knows, this meeting would never have happened!"

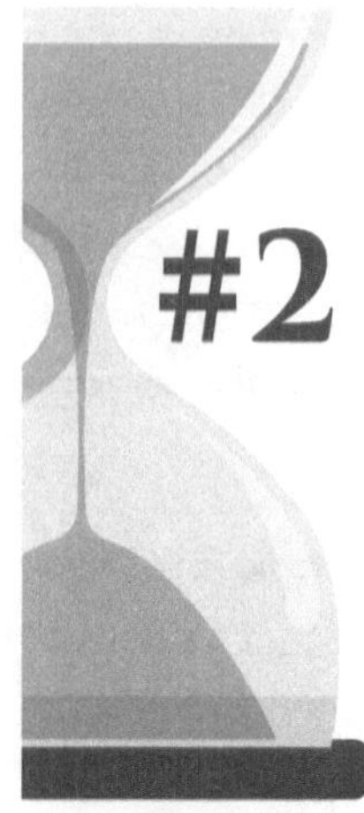

#2

January 2014

"The registrations of VigyaPun have been done," Raghav informed Disha, as he entered their new office, located at C-Scheme in Jaipur.

The office was very small, just enough to accommodate three people with their laptops, but had a high-speed internet connection and unlimited supply of coffee and tea. Basically, it had everything a startup needed. Raghav announced the completion of all statutory compliances of starting a new company, which officially meant they could start billing now. Starting with two clients, achieved through the existing network of Raghav, Disha and he worked round the clock to ensure maximum satisfaction of their clients. Digital advertising powered by technology, was still an unexplored field and an untapped market in India. The nascent stage of the sector was a roadblock and before becoming a market leader, they had to first create market awareness for themselves.

Starting from Jaipur was a strategic decision. Being the hometown of both Raghav and Disha, it served as a great place to arrange resources at cheaper cost, to have a comfortable living with low expenses and to develop the company at this seed stage. Besides, Raghav's love for the city was why he thought that the startup and business ecosystem in Tier II cities like Jaipur should grow with youngsters setting up businesses in these cities.

While Raghav handled the business development and finance end of the company, which was practically the role of a founder, Disha was responsible for the design and creative end along with the execution of projects. Raghav's phone vibrated and flashed, *Kanika Calling…'*

"Hey! You seem to be too busy. You did not reply to my texts."

"Sorry Kanika, I have been caught up with work since morning. And by the way, my company got registered! Yay!" Raghav told her, seemingly enthusiastic about it.

"Wow. That is nice, so what are your plans for lunch? It's 2.30 already!" said Kanika.

Her cold reaction and the sudden change of topic troubled Raghav.

"I am overloaded with work. You carry on; let's catch up in the evening over tea."

"Sure…" Kanika agreed and hung up.

Raghav put down his phone and thought for a few minutes. *What's wrong?*

Was he so engrossed with the setup of the new company, that he placed it above his relationship?

But this gave him genuine happiness and elated him. Having his own office, his own team, while being the sole decision maker, gave him a sense of power and responsibility that he enjoyed.

`"Dude…" Disha's voice brought him back to reality.

"Yeah!" said Raghav, sounding baffled.

"Are you okay? You seem to be lost."

"No! I am fine! Tell me?" said Raghav, sipping water.

"I need the client scope of the work document. I want to know the exact deliverables that we agreed on with the real estate firm."

"Sure!" said Raghav and mailed her the required document. For a few more minutes, they remained lost in their own laptop screens.

"You know what?" said Raghav, looking at Disha. Disha gave him a questioning look.

"We need to expand really soon, otherwise, we will be facing tough competition in the same space. I am browsing the internet and I see a lot of people are coming up with similar stuff, though not the same."

"I know,but for that, we need a team, and we don't have the money to hire people. We are only two of us, along with the few interns that we have. We cannot expand with this team, Raghav!"

"Exactly!" said Raghav, his eyes beaming, which evidently meant that he had a plan. Raghav always needed a certain push to speak so that he could make it more dramatic.

"So?" Disha enquired impatiently.

"Let us raise funding!"

"Raghav, I think you are moving too fast!" said Disha immediately, without a second thought.

"Everyone raises funds, why are you against it? No big unicorn is built without funding!"

"I agree! But why do we have to imitate or clone the unicorns? We are a proper service and analysis based company. We can create something really unique on our own!"

"You do make sense, Disha. But I don't want to become stagnant. Everywhere I read funding seems to be the fastest solution to success."

"Let us not aim to be the fastest, Raghav. Let's aim to be the best."

"Fine! I see a point in what you are saying. I think working with startups, term sheets, and investors as a consultant has narrowed my thinking. Moreover, I am very possessive about my equity," said Raghav, with a wink.

"True. But you really think this entire funding scenario is a boon?" she asked, genuinely looking to gain knowledge.

"There is no black and white in this industry, Disha. I have worked closely in this domain. Raising funds at the right time for growth purposes has given amazing results to entrepreneurs. But having said that, investors are vultures. Obviously, they do invest their hard-earned money in a company, but it is trouble when they start getting involved in day-to-day activities. That is when the real trouble starts!"

Disha nodded, trying to get a sense of what he said.

* * *

Raghav continued to work on his laptop, as he waited for Kanika at the café. A winter evening of Jaipur, an open sitting area and a quiet place for a conversation was the perfect setup. Raghav and Kanika made it a point to meet over tea or coffee in the evening, every day to spend quality time together. Kanika walked into the café and sat next to him.

Holding his hand, she said, "I am so sorry! You had to wait almost 15 minutes!"

"That is okay, baby!" said Raghav, looking into her eyes. Their relationship had been going on for 10 months now, and had been amazing. Kanika had started working right after her results of Chartered Accountancy. They had met in a consultancy company where they worked together.

Two months ago, when Raghav had decided to move on to start his own venture Kanika had openly voiced her thoughts of not being on board with the decision in principle. But seeing Raghav's passion and enthusiasm about it, she eventually decided to support him.

Their differences of opinion were fuelled by the 'secure' family background of Kanika, where they held jobs and did not have anything to do with a business. Her concerns were genuine. She was worried about Raghav deciding to leave a safe future and putting everything at stake, including his savings and of course, his relationship.

Nevertheless, like all millennial relationships, considering how their relationship had always been open and vocal, she decided to voice her concerns, but be there to support Raghav during this phase of change in his life.

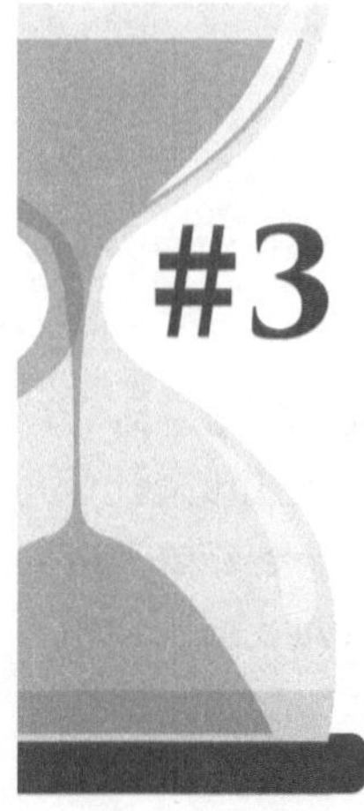

#3

January 2016

Twenty-seven years old, born in Jaipur, Raghav was a chartered accountant by degree, but had never practised as one. He had always identified as a storyteller, a content creator, or a people-person. He loved talking to people, knowing their stories and perceiving them in his own manner. This led to his decision to move on from his plush job as a senior consultant with one of the leading financial firms of the country, to take the plunge of starting an ad-tech startup.

For three years, Raghav had worked as a startup business consultant and risen up the ranks with his quick business skills, sharp intellect, acumen, and communication skills. His skills of being a people-person had worked well in his consulting career as well. Eventually, Raghav started feeling suffocated and wanted to get back to his passion of telling stories.

He felt advertising was his calling. He wanted to create an affordable, approachable solution, which could help everyone from a corporate giant to a small shopkeeper to take advantage of geo-targeted advertising and avail services of good quality content customised for their target groups and local audiences.

VigyaPun laid the foundation for this calling. With his existing network, and travelling across the country tirelessly, for over a year, VigyaPun grew to become one of the most recognized advertising startups. Being headquartered in Jaipur, Raghav's hometown, VigyaPun had gained significant traction from Tier II and III cities, and the entire Northern India.

However, the catch-22 situation started capsulating VigyaPun. Raghav wanted to grow faster. His greed for success and recognition was now insatiable. That is the thing about being an entrepreneur – there is no stopping at a particular stage. You always want more, and you want it fast.

With more than seventy-five per cent of business coming from the NCR region, majorly from New Delhi, Gurgaon, Noida and Faridabad, Raghav wanted to establish an office and hire more people there. However, it needed additional funds over the existing reserves of the company. He had never really thought about raising funds, but now he deliberated and read the literature available about it on the internet day and night.

He finally decided to raise his concerns with his most trusted cohort of people, his core team. Farukh, Disha, and Kriti, sat across Raghav with full attention.

"See, I am not very aware about this entire funding scenario. I have never been very active in this ecosystem. I think it has to be your own call, Raghav," said Farukh upfront, as he tried to understand the entire situation.

"Does that mean you will lose control over decision making? Because I am not working under anyone else's leadership," exclaimed Disha, in her ever-rebellious attitude.

Raghav laughed and tried to calm her down, "Ha! Disha, funding happens in exchange of a minority stake of the company. Obviously, we will have investors to answer and someone on the board seat as well, but that would be more of guidance and reporting. They will not have anything to do with the day-to-day working."

"You told us that the company is profitable," Kriti asked in all her innocence, seemingly losing confidence in the company she had trusted in for so many months.

"Haha! Of course, Kriti. This is growth capital that we are looking at. This is more about raising funds for rapid growth, setting up a new geography and hiring new people. We are just little over a year old and we have in fact, registered tremendous success. That is why we need this fund to continue the growth trajectory."

"See Raghav," said Disha in her authoritative tone, "It seems you are pretty confident about the fund-raise. We are all here to stand by you. If this is your decision and this is what is right for the company, let us do it."

Raghav smiled confidently about the support that his core team extended without fail. He was proud of having built a culture, where the core team had the ownership of decision-making and were a part of the entire company-building process. He had always wanted to create a team like this.

"With my network from my consulting days, I am sure we will raise the amount we are looking for. The bigger picture is that it will be time for you guys to step up and think bigger. You will need to manage new geography; train new teams and manage new clients that will be coming on board."

"I am up for the challenge, and it sounds very exciting!" exclaimed Farukh gleefully.

"Calls for a party, in that case?" shouted Raghav.

"Aye Aye, Captain!" Kriti high-fived him, as they left the office together.

Raghav started the entire process of raising funds. Numerous iterations of pitch decks, multiple sheets of different connects that he had and hundreds of numeric calculations and projections to convince investors, now filled up his laptop. He got less involved in the routine operations for a few days, as Disha and Farukh ran the show seamlessly.

As meetings started happening, Raghav realised no matter how convinced you are as a business owner, it is a whole different ball game to convince people to shell out their hard earned money for your dream.

"Why disrupt advertising? Why Jaipur? Why smaller clients in Tier II and III?"

These questions pierced Raghav's ideologies in every meeting. His vision remained stable – to create a digital advertising solution for Tier II and III, where every small and medium sized business owner could also leverage the power of digital advertising and reach their target audience more efficiently. Investors found it less lucrative to deal with smaller accounts and wanted a solution that could target bigger businesses, and thus bigger revenues. Moreover, trying to convince investors that a talented team could be built from Jaipur was another challenge.

Tier II was considered to be like a curse. As if, you belonged to a god-forsaken place with no resources. People believed that beyond certain colleges and beyond certain cities, there was no talent in India and this taboo combined with the nascent and myopic vision of the investor community was already pulling back the hundreds of young and visionary first generation entrepreneurs of the country.

As the funding scene was still maturing in India during this period, global investors pushing huge loads of money into the startup ecosystem further intensified the Tier I bias.

Raghav gave his best during these months. Rejections had hardened him and the best part to keep his mind focussed was the fact that he believed in his idea and his team. As new clients kept coming on-board, Raghav was assured of their growth trajectory no matter what. Funding was a route for him to achieve bigger things at a faster pace.

He called out to Disha from his cabin, one day in the office only to find out that she was sleeping at her desk. He immediately called her in his cabin.

"Sleeping in the office? Not that I mind, but is everything okay?" asked Raghav out of genuine concern.

"I haven't slept since a few days," said Disha, still in a slumber.

"I see you have been a bit shaky. But this whole funding fiasco has kept me on my toes. What is up with you?"

"Uh! I broke up with Kabir last week."

"What?" asked Raghav, shocked.

Disha had been going out with Kabir for more than five years. They were made for each other and it was Kabir who often picked her up from office in the evening. A sudden sense of distancing crept in Raghav. He had been emotionally unavailable for his friends, colleagues, and family for some time now. It triggered an emotion of utmost carelessness and irresponsibility.

His family, Kanika, his colleagues – everyone flashed in his mind and he realised he had not sat with anyone to have a real conversation in a while. Was he already paying the price of venturing into entrepreneurship? Were his relationships going to suffer? He immediately thought about the Work-Life Balance e-book he had found somewhere and downloaded. But ironically because of the erratic schedule, he did not get the time to read it.

"We had been at loggerheads since some time now. I have also been swept in work with new accounts and managing business development, while you have been busy. We did not get to talk much. And miscommunication often leads to an unhealthy relationship. I just could not take it anymore and we decided to end it."

Raghav felt as if the onus was on him. He realised how people working for you sometimes give so much more to your company than you realise. A team putting their personal lives at stake and giving that extra effort for the company's success means so much to an entrepreneur. He felt blessed to have found team members who he could depend on.

"Disha, I can tell you that you are a wonderful person and this hiccup should not affect you mentally. But you know this is too run of the mill. I don't want to trivialise what happened with you by asking you to just chill and move on."

Disha looked at him and gave him a wry smile.

Raghav looked at his laptop. A half-written mail was staring at him that had to be sent to one of the investors as a follow-up response. He had four other tabs open where he had on-going conversations with investors and had to revert to more queries with more data. It could take him all night. He looked at Disha who played with her fingers, still lost in her thoughts.

In a moment, Raghav shut his laptop lid and stood up. Disha looked at him because of his sudden movement.

"Let's fuck all of it. Let's go out somewhere," said Raghav with a laugh.

"But I thought you had investors to reply to."

"They can wait. We don't make our clients wait, but investors surely can!" said Raghav with a wink and nudged Disha to get up.

They walked out of the office a few minutes later.

"Raghav, this is crazy! It is a weekday and we have work pending. Where are we even going?"

"Making your weekday, LIT," said Raghav and drove faster. Disha knew in an instant. LIT was a happening club in Jaipur, one of the newly opened ones, with the millennial youth of the city thronging it, from the day it started.

They sat on the high chairs at the bar counter and ordered their first round of beers.

"So, this relationship stuff! Does it go well with you?" asked Disha, as more beers kicked in.

"I see it as a part of life," said Raghav gulping down his beer, and speaking loudly to be heard over the music. "I hope I am not sounding too much like a wannabe millennial, but it truly is just one part of the many facets of life."

"It doesn't sound anything, but yes, a bit insensitive."

"I don't know. I have seen the worst days of my life while I was trying to build this company. When we did not have a single client, but had to pay the rent from my savings. I have literally dried up everything I had and started from scratch. It just took too much to really care about trivial things."

"Trivial?" said Disha, in an arguing tone. "Relationships are trivial!"

"No! Not how I put it. But yes, I don't want to make my relationship the focal point of my life."

"Or you say that because of what is going on in your relationship currently?"

Raghav kept quiet, trying to ignore the elephant in the room, as what Disha said was actually true. He cared about his relationships. He cared about the people associated with him. But a part of him was trying to disassociate from Kanika, trying to convince himself that he was fine without her and he did not actually need this relationship in the first place.

"Do you think you rushed into this breakup?" Raghav asked Disha intuitively, probably trying to find his own answers.

"I feel it is fine. You know what, I have a theory!" said Disha and thumped the table. Raghav laughed knowing that it was one of those drunken theories.

"I have a theory that every relationship has a due course. It is like a marathon. It is bound to reach the finish line. Now it differs from person-to-person or marathon-to-marathon whether it is a 10-kilometre run or a 50-kilometre run! What do you say?" said Disha and punched him on his arm.

"Hmm!" Raghav mockingly thought. "I think that this is a bullshit theory. What do you say about the people who get married happily and live a beautiful life together?"

Disha looked down at her beer and smiled. "In my terms, they are just walking slowly in a marathon because they like it. They don't ever want to reach the finish line."

Raghav raised his eyebrow and his glass, "Wow! Cheers to that thought!"

"And you see, what happens in a marathon when you can see the finish line? You run faster towards it. So I just sprinted towards it because I could already see it," said Disha and concluded her weird theory with a laugh.

Her practicality and realism inspired Raghav. She was strong, or at least she showed it really well. He was glad he worked with people, he could learn from. Disha worked her ass off on any project or role assigned to her. Yet, she never attached herself emotionally to anything so that it could hurt her. She could move on in life – from anything and that was a quality one cannot build easily.

As Raghav looked at his watch to keep a tab on the time, Disha said, finishing her last drink, "You know what, Raghav?"

"Yeah?"

"This company and my work keep me going. I might sound selfish, but this is my self-defence. I work harder to shut out everything else in the world. I want to reach somewhere, achieve something, and be someone without any prejudice or bias. No family name, no fathers' pressure, no marriage pulling me down. I want to be on my own. I cannot let a Kabir decide for me, if I should work all night or not! I cannot let a man decide if I have to get married or not, even if he is my father."

Raghav realised it was deeper than it looked. He did not want to probe further, as he could see it was a Pandora's Box of her feelings.

"And you know why I work in this company and why I cannot put anything above it?"

"You tell me…" Raghav said cautiously.

"Because you let me be 'me'. You don't dictate what I should do 'as a girl'. Or for that matter, you don't dictate to any of us. You respect everyone the way they are and that is what makes all the difference."

❊ ❊ ❊

One year into the company, with strong finances and growth trajectory, VigyaPun raised the first round of funds with the objective of hiring across Jaipur and New Delhi, and expanding its reach further into Southern India.

With the New Delhi office opening up, Raghav developed a strong base in the capital city and rented a flat in the fast upcoming and relatively quiet Charmwood Village of Faridabad. Situated comfortably on the Delhi-Faridabad border, Charmwood was a peaceful neighbourhood, just a few minutes away from South Delhi and quiet enough not to experience the rush and pollution of Delhi.

The Delhi stint treated Raghav really well. While the company touched new heights under his leadership and the new team, the revenue quadrupled in little over a year. The Delhi branch started churning out seventy-five per cent of the company's revenues and the team grew to over sixty people working full time. During this time, Raghav started diving deeper into his work life, with erratic timing schedules and a workaholic lifestyle. House parties with colleagues, investor meetings, legal compliances, and regular business development became more frequent.

Raghav had never been happier, living the life he had always wanted. Hustling between two of his favourite cities of Jaipur and New Delhi, managing both office locations, and creating a company with unimaginable sweat, passion and love was something he had always dreamt of.

As happy as he was at work, his relationship with Kanika had never been shakier.

"Drishti and Farukh are coming over again?" Kanika asked Raghav, as they sat across the sofa in the living room of Raghav's house. The quaint lighting of the room and the aroma of fresh air after the winter rain filled the house. Raghav often kept the balcony door open on rainy evenings to make the most out of the 10th floor apartment.

"Yeah! You know they both live at a stone's throw. Plus, they don't have anyone here as well. It rained today, and we decided to chat over a few drinks and chill, while we were wrapping up the day in the office."

"Raghav, I get one weekend off from work! I wanted to spend it alone with you," Kanika snapped at him. She had her own apartment closer to her office in Noida, but she came over for weekends at Raghav's place. Kanika's company had transferred her to Delhi, because of a recent promotion.

"And so do I, Kanika. I cannot just abandon my team. They have moved their residences to new cities for me. They live alone here, working for VigyaPun day and night."

"Not for free, Raghav!"

"That is insensitive. This is the time when we can strengthen the team bond and put together a stellar core team for a lifetime. We are friends; we are like a family here in Delhi."

"And you are the messiah of all!" Kanika mocked Raghav. "We hardly talk, Raghav."

"Have you ever thought of the reason behind that? Maybe because you are so full of yourself that you do not want to hear about my work or my company at all!"

An awkward silence followed as they looked at each other with dead lifeless eyes.

"Raghav, things were so much better a few months ago."

"Be specific, Kanika. You mean, when I was in a job!"

"Fine! Yes! You have anyway lost all your savings on setting up a business and now you are risking our relationship as well."

Raghav shook his head and buried his face in his palms. He went to the balcony for a quiet moment, alone, and lit up a cigarette. The smoke created a thick cloud in the rainy weather, as the cool breeze hit his face. He took a few deep breaths.

Winter has something extremely silent about it. On the 10th floor of the building, it felt even more distant from the rest of the world. He stared into the dead abyss. He could not defend himself for letting his relationship slip out of his hands so easily, but at the same time, he knew Kanika was not the right person to stay with at this juncture of his life. She would not understand his life choices and would never be able to come to terms with the fact that he was on to doing something of his own.

He could not afford to be with someone, who was waiting for him to fail so that they could deliver the 'I told you so' speech. As an entrepreneur, you think about that speech every day – expecting it to drop from your parents, partner, or colleagues. He dreaded that moment of failure. Witnessing the rise and breakthroughs that VigyaPun had achieved in the last few months, he did not want any negative thoughts around him.

But was it right to shut yourself away from people like this? Was he being unreasonable and expecting something wrong from a partner? After all, a secure future is what everyone looks for. But why is a man always expected to provide that secure future? While society has undermined and neglected the power and strength of women for a long time, it has also wrongly expected too much of the same out of men, thus creating an imbalance.

These random thoughts played the devil's advocate in Raghav's mind, as he continued standing in the balcony with his dead stare.

"I should not have said that..." said Kanika meekly, as she joined him on the balcony.

"Kanika, this company is all that I have. I have built it from scratch. I have exploited my entire network, traveling across the country to get the first set of clients. We have raised funds and we are creating something big around here in the world of advertising. This is exciting for me; this gives me the thrill that

I had never imagined earlier," Raghav spoke without stopping for breath.

"I respect that, Raghav. But this is just a 'business', after all. What if this is not successful? You don't have a business family to fall back on. What if it fails like ninety per cent of the startups do?"

Raghav smiled at her. He looked in the far distance at the empty fields adjacent to his building. This balcony had been one of the main reasons he had chosen this apartment.

"But what if it survives, like the ten per cent?" he asked with a smile.

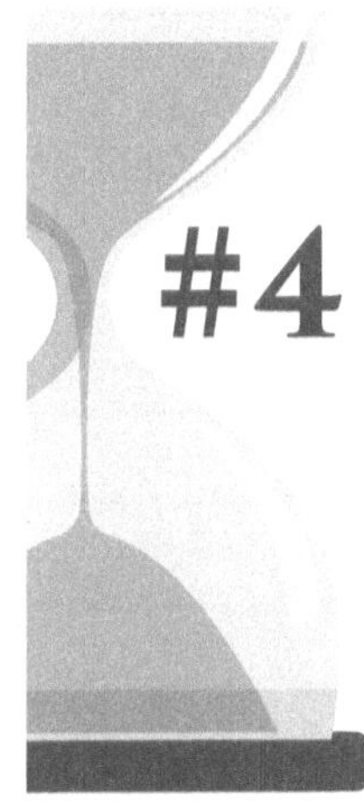

#4

October 2016

Kanika placed her cup of tea softly on the table. Thoughtfully staring at the opposite wall in a quaint café of Jaipur, she said almost in a whisper, "And this is your final decision?"

Kanika had started maintaining a distance. Raghav could sense this, all through this time anyway that she did not approve of his choice of plunging into entrepreneurship, risking the security net of a well-settled job and being so immersed into work. Despite all his efforts to meet her, spend more time with her, the distance grew. The relationship had become more of a tag for them and they realised that.

That's the problem with millennial relationships. Once you are in your comfort zone, breaking up seems to be a tough task, bringing unnecessary upheaval and emotional unsettlement that no one has time for. They kept dragging out because of the fear of that change in the status quo. Inertia was the only factor keeping them together.

The distance was now evident in their relationship and they finally decided to meet, after not having kept in touch for a few weeks. It was more of a closure meeting rather than a resolution one. You already know the fate of such meetings even before they happen.

After continued trouble and a prolonged distance, they decided to take that step. Raghav thought it was necessary to let this go, so Kanika could find someone to fulfil her checklist. They often planned their trips to their hometown Jaipur so they could travel together. This was now a coincidence that they were both in Jaipur on the same weekend, despite not having spoken for over a month.

That's how they decided to meet at their old time favourite tea cafe. Kanika had not put much effort in dressing up, seemingly because it was a Sunday morning, or maybe, because she did not want to put that effort any more for Raghav.

She found Raghav unreasonably diving deeper into a risky venture with no backing of a family business or a secure job with retirement plans. That was not who Raghav was.

In the last few months, there had been weeks when they had not even talked to each other. The millennial fear of an emotional outbreak had kept them from speaking about it. Deep down, they knew that the relationship was long dead.

Raghav had ordered his staple honey ginger tea—now almost cold, untouched, and neglected. Kanika sipped her cup of masala chai several times—but only to break the silence, with the nervous tapping of her fingers on the table.

Finally, not able to take Raghav's silent treatment any more, Kanika spoke again stronger than before, "Raghav, tell me! Is this shift your final decision?"

Raghav looked at her, seemingly troubled and nodded silently. Kanika looked down and placed her hand on the cup of tea three times, possibly confused about picking it up.

"Raghav, you don't have to do this! Jaipur is a great place for business and the opportunities are growing constantly," Kanika tried to sound logical.

"Kanika, it is a board decision!"

"Raghav, it is your company, for God's sake!" She raised her voice, almost helplessly.

Raghav looked at her, staring into the depth of her eyes reminding himself of the last two years. He felt partially guilty for how he had put his relationship at stake, to give more time to his venture. But was it really something to be guilty of?

"It is a 10 million USD valued, investor funded company, Kanika. I am answerable to the board," Raghav told her. Suddenly, lowering his voice almost in guilt, he added, "And I believe this is the best decision in the interest of the company. We need to expand aggressively. This is what I have always wanted."

"You can hire people in London to head the UK business and travel there to oversee the operations. Why do you have to relocate completely?" said Kanika, now sounding close to tears.

"Kanika, this is my company, my brainchild. I have to manage finances and business development for the entire UK unit. It's a hands on job needing close monitoring on a day-to-day basis. I cannot do that from Jaipur." Raghav placed his hand on Kanika's wrist and continued, "Are you sure it is only about my decision to move to London? Won't the same thing happen if it was Delhi or Bangalore for that matter?"

"Raghav, you know the situation, right? My parents are already bent upon my marriage and it is already hard explaining to them why I love a startup guy! You going away for an undecided time period to a place so far away is not going to help the situation."

"Kanika…"

"Raghav I am asking you again, is your decision final?"

"Kanika, are you doing this just because you never wanted me to take the entrepreneurial plunge?"

"Ha!" Kanika smirked sarcastically. "As if you would have cared about what I feel, anyway."

Raghav looked down staring at his untouched cup of tea. He had thousands of thoughts running in his mind and hundreds of words that he wanted to say. But he could not utter a word.

He did not know whether to feel guilty or helpless. Had he brought this relationship to this stage? Was it because of his startup? Was it an expensive sacrifice that he was making for his company? Was starting his own business and being passionate about it so much of a crime?

"Kanika, I have tried everything that I can to keep you happy and work things out in this relationship, while building this company from scratch."

"Raghav, it was not an obligation! You had a seventy-lakh per fucking annum of a job offer at hand, which you shoved in the dustbin without even asking me!" Kanika picked up her purse and took out a fifty rupees note, which was evidently her share of the bill.

"This is over, Raghav. We are done!"

With those few words, she walked out of the café, leaving Raghav to watch her go until she was out of sight.

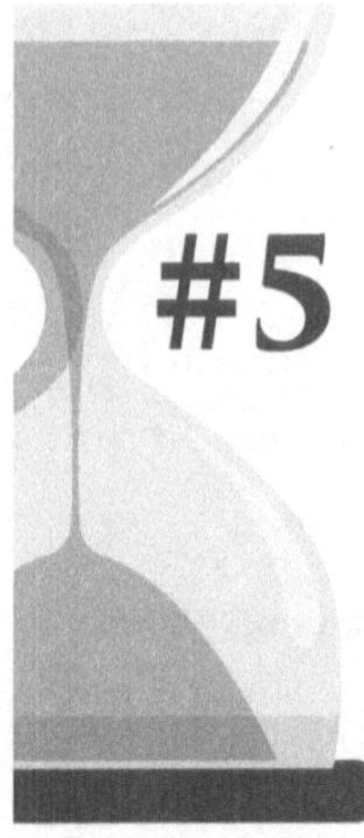

October 2016

After the meeting, Raghav now made peace with the fact that maybe the relationship was not meant for him, at least at the moment. During the next seven days of his separation with Kanika, Raghav engrossed himself in work. He doubled his efforts on his expansion plans and drowned his feelings into the sea of work. That is who Raghav was. He did feel a pinch of guilt about how he moved on so easily, but then he convinced himself that they had known the fate of the relationship for almost a year now. Another problem with millennial relationships is that they are too easy to fall into, and too easy to fall out of.

Raghav had been preparing for his trip to London during this week. He tried making a few connections over LinkedIn, reaching out to a couple of people and also finding places to stay on AirBnB. After some frantic searches, he realised he was too late for a city too big and he had to zero in on a final place to stay as soon as possible.

The move to London had been strategic. With the investor

pressure mounting to expand the service area and increase revenue margins, Raghav had thought a lot. With his line of business, Asia could be easily managed with a strong team based in India, but outside Asia, Europe seemed to be his next choice for business. Brexit had changed many business scenarios in the area, creating unprecedented challenges and Raghav had a personal feeling that it could be a good time to set up an advertising arm in London considering that it had plenty of potential in the current scheme of things.

With a mind full of questions and deliberations, Raghav sat alone in the balcony of Hauz Khas Social in New Delhi. Overlooking the not-so-fresh lake of Hauz Khas, Raghav often liked to spend his evenings with his laptop and a drink at a place like this. Since his breakup, he had guiltily been enjoying his alone time. Such evenings gave him a lot of space to think.

Ironically, as he thought about the sheer pleasure of his alone time, he heard a voice right behind him, "Raghav!"

He turned around. Getting up from his chair, extending his hand for a polite handshake, Raghav tried to recollect and place the girl in his memory. Unoffended, she happily confirmed, "This is Jasleen, from The Startup Stories."

Raghav immediately connected. The Startup Stories was one of the most popular print as well as digital news platforms in the country. It was the Filmfare in the world of startups and Jasleen was their star correspondent, the face of the media platform.

Jasleen had once done a feature on Raghav and after spending plenty of time on the interaction, had titled it, *'The Starry-eyed*

Tier II Boy, making his mark in the NCR.'

Raghav had not liked the headline and the spicy narrative that was built around it. He had always loathed the Tier I and Tier II divide, and the bias surrounding it.

Since then, he had stayed away from The Startup Stories. Raghav avoided clashes, as he knew that his dark sarcastic remarks were bound to hurt someone. Thus, he steered clear. Recently, Jasleen had tried to reach him, wanting to do a follow up story about his London expansion. But he did not want her to break the story, with her biased attempts of creating click bait stories.

Jasleen sat next to Raghav and lit a cigarette. She was in no mood to back off this time.

"So, what has been up with you? I thought you had an office in Faridabad!" said Jasleen, looking around jokingly.

"Ha! I just like..." said Raghav and hesitantly added, "my alone time."

Jasleen ignored the remark, of course.

"Tell me, Raghav! Let us do a follow up story. How has it been going for you in Delhi now? You have been the spotlight in the startup circles, dude."

"Uh! Have I? And right now might not be the best time for the story?"

"I am sure you have got time..." said Jasleen pointing at Raghav's glass which was almost completely full. " Moreover, any time is a good time for a story."

Raghav sighed and took a sip from his drink, cursing under his breath.

"So tell me, how has Delhi treated you? I see you all around in keynote sessions, mentorship panels, and advertising conferences!"

Raghav put on his fake smile and tried to transform into his sparkling demeanour. As an entrepreneur dealing with hundreds of people every day, you need the control over the switch of your mood and personality. This made him a people's person.

"Yes, it has been a roller coaster ride. Amidst the entire hustle of setting up and expanding operations, I have been getting invites to events and sessions, which is humbling. And it is always good to interact and network with people, sharing their stories."

"And how does it feel as someone from a Tier II town, to make your mark in Delhi? Is it more challenging?"

Raghav shook his head with visible dissatisfaction. His demeanour was failing him. In his fairly calm aggression, he said, "Tier II, III… all this is a state of mind, Jasleen. You can be a Tier II or III person even in Delhi or Mumbai, as long as you have a narrow thinking. Anyone anywhere can make it big, and the city has got nothing to do with it. Opportunities don't come knocking at your door because you are in Delhi."

"Uh! I didn't mean to sound like that, Raghav."

"I am sure. The starry-eyed Tier II boy is not a tag. It shows how myopic you are as a person."

"That headline was approved by the editors as well. I thought that was the best way to portray the inspirational story."

"Maybe I am taking the wrong offense. Or actually, I am not even offended at this. I am not here in this city, with a starry-eyed dream of making it big. This is only a step for us as a company, in our journey to spread across. Jaipur is and will always be VigyaPun's home."

"And do you think you will be able to make a bigger brand with the baggage of being from a Tier II city?"

Raghav stayed silent for a few seconds and sipped his drink. He was not mad at Jasleen for asking this. Maybe the reason he was so hurt after all, was that it was true. He debated inside himself.

"Why can't bigger companies come from smaller cities?" Raghav asked, more to himself.

"Maybe because of the lack of network, exposure and talent pool— most people leave their hometowns because of lack of opportunities. See, maybe that is why you are in this whole conundrum of thinking that you are still a company from Jaipur, while your entire core team including you, is stationed in Delhi right now."

"But someone has to break that cycle. Younger millennials don't want to stay in Jaipur because of lack of opportunities and companies don't set up there because of lack of exposure and talent pool. This vicious loop has to be broken."

"But why didn't you break this loop? You could have kept Jaipur as your permanent HQ and travelled around for business."

"Uh! Our investors…" said Raghav and then looked at Jasleen suspiciously. She immediately understood and said in a jiffy, "I am not writing anything down. I promise. I speak as a friend."

Raghav smiled at her. "There are a lot of responsibilities and changes that come with raising funds. The investors would not want a PR of being invested in a small town startup. They want a pie of the bigger picture, riding on our back. They wanted us to have an office in Delhi and then wanted our entire core team of four people to be in Delhi as well."

"Everyone has their own reason, Raghav. Tier II is treated like a curse even today. You think my headline was biased? I am from Lucknow, Raghav. But four years ago, when I came here, for months I was considered fit for writing in only Hindi, just because of my background. No doubt, my Hindi was also fairly good, but I wanted to write on startups and technology in English. That was my language of study. That is how ruthless this entire system is."

"Fair enough. I have my own helpless reasons."

"True. Also, do you really think staying in Jaipur would have helped you grow at this scale?"

"I want to do business across the globe. But my heart remains in Jaipur. I wanted to build this from Jaipur."

Raghav went in his own deep thoughts with that. As he silently got back to his laptop, Raghav thought about the decision of relocating to Delhi.

This is temporary. As soon as we are set, I will be back. He thought to himself. But that is what every millennial leaving his hometown thought. He reflected on what Kanika had said. He actually *had* sacrificed a lot for this startup, and relationship was the least concerning at this moment.

While these thoughts raced through his mind, he suddenly remembered something. Stopping immediately, he searched for a contact on his phone and walked away from the noise.

"Hello Mr Skelton. What if I tell you, we can automate all your advertising efforts on a single dashboard with data analysis that could help you generate more business leads, and lower your conversion time on leads?"

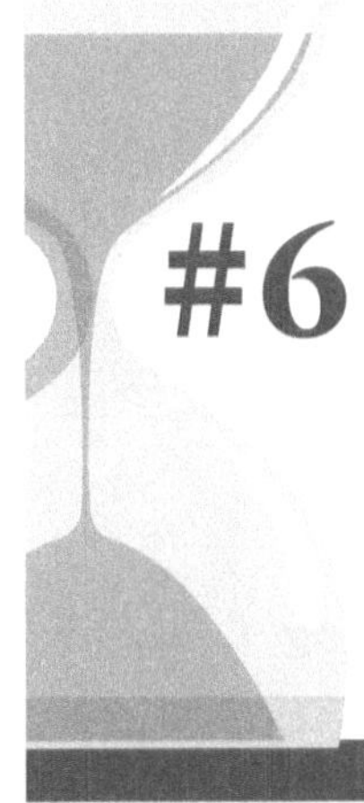

#6

The towering London Bridge
And the whiff of Thames
The beginning of an era
Or unending games

November 2016

The flight to London was surprisingly pleasant for Raghav. Three Bollywood movies, three wholesome in-flight meals, and the plane touched down with the screech of the runway. With the long process of immigration, baggage claim, and unending walks, Raghav finally found himself in the iconic London Tube's Piccadilly Line.

London had something uncannily familiar about it. The intense January cold, the calm on every person's face, the smiles exchanged; the freshness of the atmosphere and the liveliness of the surroundings made his 9 a.m. Tube journey worthwhile. He observed every bit of what was visible to his eyes, as if he had to live every second of it.

This city will have something good to offer, he thought to himself.

After a 90-minute journey and changing the Tube line once, he reached his destination. Canning Town was a part of East London, a quieter part of London as such and one of the fast developing ones. He entered the AirBnB he had finally chosen; it was just as he had imagined his workstation for the next two weeks to be!

Nestled away on the 8th floor of the building, the studio apartment had a plush wooden-floored balcony, a modern modular kitchen and the perfect modern amenities that he had wished for. A very high speed uninterrupted Wi-Fi, needless to say, was a huge plus for an Indian. The balcony overlooked a part of the River Thames, which was the northern end of it on one side, and the other side in the far distance was the picturesque Central London, straight out-of-the-book elements of London Eye and The Shard.

Without basking in the glory of his choice of apartment, he immediately switched on his laptop to get to work. No rest for the wicked! The time was limited and he had to make it worthwhile. The feeling of being in a land far away from home was both exciting and scary, in a weird way. In all these years of entrepreneurship, he had made a name for himself in the advertising industry. Several controversial, straight from the heart interviews, some huge PR stunts of partnerships, and some widely popular campaigns had earned him a place on the map of the industry. VigyaPun had landed some of the biggest clients in India, in a very short span of time.

However, he could not ride on the same PR wave or popularity in London. It was as if starting from scratch in a place, where no one cared who you are. Except one.

Craig Skelton was one of the most riveting entrepreneurs of the UK. With several awards and accolades under his belt, his company Creton Solutions was only 5 years old, but had risen to be the fastest growing cloud-based workforce management company. From pay scales to taxes, from transport management to vehicle tracking in real-time, from CRM to customer support software, Creton Solutions provided end-to-end management of the entire workforce to over 800 organizations, in the UK alone.

Raghav had met Craig Skelton at a Logistics-Tech event in Singapore, a year ago. They had a very short introduction of about five minutes and Craig had rushed off, which had seemed very arrogant to Raghav back then. Digging further into the company, Raghav realised that the founder of a company with forty million pounds of annual revenues within five years of inception, deserved to have the attitude he carried. Moreover, a business so deeply into the B2B industry was never the right target for Raghav, so he had not given the brusque meeting much thought.

Raghav looked back in time to that meeting, and then his call last week. Craig had surprisingly been kind enough to give him a 20-minute slot on his calendar, after hearing that Raghav's solution could help him automate his marketing efforts to the extent that it could capture and re-target leads that have up to 85-90% chance of conversion.

Raghav had already worked on a deck to pitch to Craig. He finished it and checked out the route to his office. Raghav walked down to the nearest Canning Town Tube Station again. London seemed to be rubbing off on him. He felt fresh despite his long journey, then the Tube ride and settling into his AirBnB. The extremely cold breeze brushed off his face. He felt chills down his spine despite his overcoat. He lit a smoke while he walked, thinking about how his life had taken a spin in the last couple of days.

From a breakup to a new country, altogether, and yet he did not have time to take a moment and let it all sink in. He loved the pace of his life, but sometimes, he felt that he missed the chance to stop and smell the roses. The company needed to increase the revenues rapidly and that was all that kept his mind occupied. Sometimes, he did feel the need of a relationship, of that special someone who understood his sentiments, his entrepreneurial dreams and what he really was. But, he did not want to be curtailed.

He boarded the train that went straight to the epochal London Bridge. As he came out of the underground tube station, the breath-taking view and the surroundings swept him off his feet for a minute. It was too much to grasp. The mere grandeur of The Tower Bridge suavely standing tall, the happening pace of people around and the essence of being alive was spellbinding. The cloudy, pinching cold weather added to the typical London beauty.

He started walking following the map directions towards the office. The swanky buildings, with hundreds and thousands of people having beers, smoking and eating all around added to the entire hustle of the city. A mix of tourists, who looked as amazed as Raghav, and locals, who went on with their lives seeming to be the happiest lot ever, was an overwhelming experience.

He entered the tower that loomed diagonally opposite London Bridge. Raghav thought, *'must be one of the most expensive locations in the world for an office'*. Entering his details on a tablet and getting a Visitor Pass generated, Raghav reached the fourth floor of the building and entered the office, which proudly bore the words 'Creton Solutions' right behind the reception desk. Within minutes, Raghav was being escorted inside, marvelling at the well-oiled working of Craig's office. Inside was a sea of people. Lined up with cabins and conference rooms on one side of the aisle, and hundreds of hot desks on the other, the vastness of the office intimidated him, but he maintained his composure.

He did not have to wait. The meeting was bang on schedule without a minute's delay. Everyone he passed in the aisle greeted him with a smile. Is it a thing with more developed and progressive countries? You tend to become courteous and graceful as a society, with development.

Sell. Sell. Sell. He repeated inside his head like a mantra. The wall right outside the huge cabin read, **"If you are not selling, what good are you?"**

Arrogance reeked in the quote, but maybe that is what it takes to build a company of this scale, Raghav thought to himself. With a hundred thoughts in his mind, he stepped inside the cabin.

"Hello Sir. Hope you are doing well today!" Craig exclaimed in a thick British accent, as he shook his hand.

"All well, Craig. Hope you are good too," replied Raghav, as he took the seat opposite Craig.

"You want to quickly take me through what you can do for us?"

"Of course!" said Raghav. It was his moment. He took a deep breath. This moment could turn things around for his company. **If you are not selling, what good are you?** The quote resounded in his mind before he began.

In the next 12 minutes, Raghav explained how varied and distributed marketing efforts of Creton Solutions could be integrated on one platform, along with strong Search Engine Optimisation and Marketing tools. With the use of artificial intelligence and data analytics, people of the right level of seniority could be reached across different touch points and it could all be integrated into one common lead funnel on a single dashboard with multiple user facilities. Results? Almost 65% saving in time and up to 30-40% saving in marketing cost. Plus, 80% more authenticity of leads being generated with a 95% chance of conversion.

"You offer a workforce management solution. You ask other businesses to outsource their workflow management to your software, because it is not their core business function to do it. Similarly, marketing is not your core, Craig. You are awesome at workflow management. I am awesome at automating advertising. Let us do what we are best at!" Raghav closed and gulped down a glass of water, waiting to bounce off Craig's reaction.

Craig was quiet. It made Raghav uncomfortable to not be able to read his thoughts. Raghav had always been overconfident about his observational skills. Craig was unreadable at the moment.

"Mr Sharma," Craig said again in an almost incomprehensible accent. "I would like to tell you a few experiences very quickly. We tried outsourcing to a couple of agencies a year ago. We have an advertising budget running close to 3 million pounds."

Raghav shifted a little in his seat on hearing the number, but tried not to reveal it on his face. If this deal closed, this one client would be at least hundred times their current biggest client.

"The experiences were not good as people overcommitted and were not able to deliver. In the last five months, we tried to build an in-house advertising team. But I have to admit, as you rightly said, it's not our core and the team could not function at their best productive levels considering there was no leadership."

Raghav nodded with an understanding look.

"Before you stepped in, I did my own homework on your company. I like how you have scaled up in a short span of time and with the entire solution that you have to offer. However…"

Raghav sat straight. This word 'However' had many endings, which were generally not good.

"Why do you think I should have you do it, and not some advertising tech solution from London?"

Raghav smiled softly. "Technology doesn't have a language and creativity doesn't have geography, Craig. We combine the two. Yes, we might not understand London as much as a company from London might do. But, I understand businesses.

And what I understand about yours is that you have built it with your sweat, passion and undying hard work, putting everything at stake. I know it, because I have done the same."

In the flow of the conversation and the mere mention of building a business, Raghav got carried away. He got up, buttoned up his overcoat and said, "Trust me, Craig; I know what has gone into this business. I will take care of this as much as you have. Our association is not about my product or the results. It is about trust and belief that an entrepreneur can place in another." Raghav had completely forgotten that this was an unknown land, a country a lot more professional and straightforward. He had spoken as if it was a true Indian sales meeting. Desi, to be precise. The kick of sales had overtaken him. He picked up his phone placed on the table.

"Our product saves sixty-five per cent of your time. I respect your time and 20 minutes are over," said Raghav and extended a hand for a handshake. Craig looked at him flabbergasted. He smiled and shook his hand.

As Raghav prepared to leave with a follow-up plan for this meeting, already building in his head, Craig called out, "Raghav."

Raghav stopped and turned around.

"Two months. Show me what you have. If you fuck up in these two months, there is no second chance. But if you prove that your product is as strong as your words, remember I handle more than 900 businesses, as we speak. I have 900 potential leads for you, who listen to me when I speak."

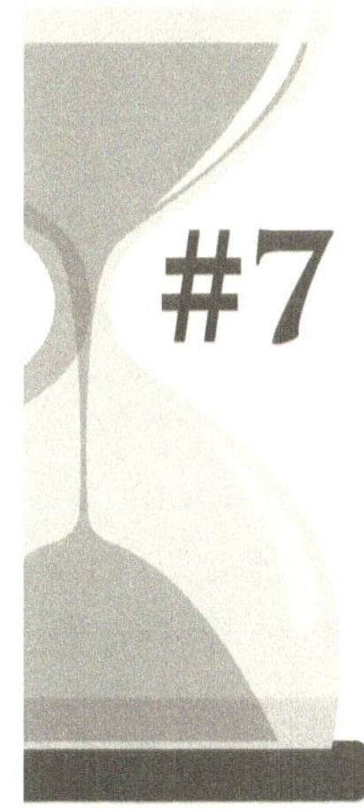

#7

It was 9 pm, by the time Raghav finished a long walk alongside the River Thames. He decided to have a quick pasta at a riverside busy cafe to satiate his screeching stomach to prepare himself for a 35 minutes Tube ride back to his flat.

It was pitch dark outside, but the liveliness of London kept it lit up. With a glass of Jack Daniel's Tennessee Honey and a smoke, Raghav stood in the balcony. Quaint, peaceful yet full of life. The London Eye was now lit up in red in the far distance. The Shard looked vibrant and one could imagine the parties and the glamour inside from miles away. Down on the street, it was busier than you would expect at this hour in India. On the street, buses, cabs, and cars rushed past in an extremely organised manner. People walked at a pace double of what you would expect after a day's work. The city had a mission. Everyone had something to look forward to. It was infectious.

Raghav sipped his bourbon, as he thought about the day and the move. He was transported back to the day he had decided to expand to London. He had just ended his relationship and he felt guilty about not giving it a second thought. However, it did not feel like a big sacrifice at the moment. As the night seemingly got darker and colder in London, he decided to connect back to the human world, coming out of his stream of thoughts.

He took out his phone and opened his chats without any particular plan in mind. The weird thing about being single in the tech-driven world is that you suddenly do not know what to do with multiple apps on your phone. He refreshed his social media feeds multiple times and opened his chats again. One of the 'frequently contacted' chat boxes popped up.

"Get the dashboards ready. You have our first UK client to handle now :)" He typed and sent it to Disha.

She had been a rock solid support in his journey of building VigyaPun all these years. Technically the first employee of the company, Disha had stuck around and built the company from scratch. Starting initially as a UI Designer and Creative Head, she had grown to handle operations, servicing, marketing, and even business development, when times had demanded. Raghav had always considered her to be more of a co-founder, rather than an employee.

"Cheers to your hard work and dedication, Raghav. I always knew we would reach here. But many more to come!" She replied. Raghav took a deep breath. It was an amazing feeling of contentment knowing that there were people to always have his back.

He typed another message – "Cracked our first UK client. Very big-ticket account. Need to set up a call." He sent it to Pradeep Kapoor.

Pradeep was the lead investor and Board Member of VigyaPun. One of the first people to come on board, Pradeep had believed in the idea before it saw the light of the day. Lately, Raghav had felt very suffocated discussing things with the entire investor pool, considering that their control and interference in the day-to-day working was increasing. In the wake of things, Pradeep had been the one to stand with Raghav against sixteen other angel investors and let him run the show in his way.

"Congrats! Four other investors will join the call. They have been insisting. Let's do 10 am London Time tomorrow. Enjoy London!" Pradeep's message beeped in the notifications.

Raghav felt a little pissed. As a founder with a consulting background, he sometimes felt disappointed in people not trusting his ways. But that was the startup ecosystem. Investors starting to meddle with day-to-day affairs, would mean that you are doing good and everyone wants a piece of the cake you are baking. At the same time, a part of Raghav would tell him to calm down, considering that, these were the people who had put their hard-earned money on his idea in the early stages.

Loud reminder tones of his phone woke Raghav up. Startled, he checked out his phone. The investor call was in 15 minutes. He looked at the time and wondered what had kept him sleeping so late. Raghav was used to waking up at seven in the morning.

Fuck Mr Jack Daniels. He thought to himself, as he gulped down two glasses of water and prepared to be grilled even more than in his meeting with Craig yesterday. Internal selling my ass.

"Are you prepared to handle an account like this, Raghav?" one of the investors asked in an intense tone.

"Yes, why not. We have the teams in place; we have the talent."

"But this is a UK client. You will need an account manager at the forefront to be the face."

I know this! You guys were the ones forcing us to go overseas in the first place! Raghav thought to himself, but kept quiet, as two of the investors talked among themselves.

"Guys, I think Raghav must already have a plan if we have come this far. Let us hear his thoughts before we give ours," Pradeep interrupted and instilled some sense in the conversation to save it from devolving into a battle of egos.

"We will need a team of at least five, to start with. I have worked that out. It would be an additional expense of around two crores in INR during this calendar year. The account of Creton Solutions would suffice for the time being, but we will need to develop other clients here rapidly to be able to sustain in the long term. In the worst case scenario, even if we fuck up Creton, we have around two to three months' time for setting up things."

"So, there is a chance that you will fuck up Creton," one of the investors was quick to pick this up.

"Umm. There is always a chance that things will get fucked up. That is why there is the term 'worst case scenario.'"

Raghav's curt reply resulted in 20 seconds of awkward silence. Pradeep was the first one to fill in.

"Raghav, you focus on starting work on the Creton account on priority. It should not be delayed. He has given you 15 days of on-boarding time. Let us first put all our energies into achieving that."

"But Pradeep, we need to think ahead. I think we need to raise funds," said an investor.

"Of course, we need to raise more funds," another one supported.

"Sir, we are already diluted enough. I strongly believe we continue relying on revenues and focus on our team strength and all your networks on building business, rather than raising further funds," Raghav quickly added. In his mind, he thought that this must be the first conversation in the world, where the founder spoke against raising funds. But, his financial instincts and business ideologies had always stopped him from raising funds after his first idea-stage round.

As expected his reply did not go down well.

"That will be for the board to decide, Raghav. We will do a consensus and make a decision."

Raghav disconnected the call in disbelief and disappointment.

Uh! This is MY company. I do not want more investor intervention! He thought to himself and gulped down his thoughts with another glass of water.

#8

"So, a multi-million dollar startup, eh?" Keshav beamed, as he sipped his beer.

The next few days in London had been exciting for Raghav. The city consumed him like one of its own and he got used to switching tubes, long walks, playing mobile games during the tube journeys and catching up on social media during bus rides. Several meetings in impressive buildings and a walk down to the iconic Tower Bridge from London Bridge every other day had made Raghav very comfortable with the vibe of the city. Standing beneath the overwhelming structure of Tower Bridge overlooking the River Thames on one side and the hustle of corporate London the other side was breath-taking.

An evening before his last evening in London, Raghav decided to catch up with an old school friend. As they stood outside the Duke of York pub in the upmarket Mayfair for a smoke, Keshav quizzed him about VigyaPun in great detail and awe.

Keshav had been a backbencher like Raghav for the last two years of their school life. They had been in touch on and off, especially in times of need, and had always been very good friends. That is the thing about some school friendships. You might not talk for months, but when you do, it's the last bench of the classroom again.

"Enough about the overhyped startup ecosystem and the vultures of the funding scene, man!" Raghav said, genuinely done with the startup talks all around him. "You tell me! How is your IT Sales treating you?"

"Same old! The economy is going down plus Brexit has severely affected our company's business. I might be looking to shift to Europe sometime soon."

"Really? Is it that bad?"

"Uh, it sucks quite a bit. Businesses are cutting down their costs rapidly, laying off employees and what not! Fuck, this discussion makes me want to light another one," said Keshav with a wry smile, lighting up another smoke. Raghav returned his plain smile, worried about his entire discussion with the investors. Thousands of thoughts reared their head in his mind.

"Fuck all this shit, bro! Tell me, how is Kanika?"

"Now you will make me light another one! We broke up a couple of days ago."

"Saw it coming! You sounded miserable the last time we Skyped. But what really happened?"

"You know most of it. I guess she never expected me to start my own thing or take this supposedly 'risky' path of entrepreneurship."

"Really? We all knew you would do something of your own!"

"So did she! But I think she never imagined that I would walk the talk. She wanted something else out of me. Job security, piles of savings, future investments even at 25 years of age!"

"She said that to you?" asked Keshav with a mocking laugh.

"She actually did!"

"Uh! Poor girl didn't see you coming."

"If that is supposed to be a double meaning dirty joke, it sucked!" said Raghav, slapping Keshav on his back as they shared a laugh.

"Anyway, now what? You wouldn't be single, I am sure!"

"For now, I am," said Raghav, seemingly comfortable. "I don't think I have the time to adjust anyone in my life right now. After this Kanika fiasco, I feel as if I won't be the right person for any girl! Who wants an entrepreneur, anyway?"

"That is so not true! You are just being under confident or modest, I do not know. But someone who understands you and your dreams would love to be with you."

"You are just a very good friend," said Raghav, as he hugged his decade-old friend.

"No, I mean it. I mean, there is no reality in a relationship if she does not understand you. She would be an opportunist if she stuck with you only when you were doing something that suited her convenience."

"That might be a bit harsh. She had her reasons. Plus, I might not have given too much to the relationship in the last few months."

"Raghav, there is no such thing as 'giving' in a relationship. It is a superficial relationship if you have to think about giving, in the first place. It has to be natural. You don't have to make an effort. Uh, how do I explain..." Keshav continued like an Agony Aunt.

Raghav smiled, "I get your point..."

Keshav cut him off, "So you know, with your parents, for example. Do you have to ever think about giving anything to them on purpose? Or do you feel obligated to do something for them? You are just there, being yourself and they don't expect anything more. The biggest thing is that they let you be!"

"You are right. And that is the notion I had about building an ideal relationship as well. Like everyone, I wish for someone smart, witty, matching with me on an intellectual level, but above all, someone who can just let me be."

"See! And Raghav let us accept the fact that it will need someone really eccentric to cope up with an entrepreneur like you!" said Keshav, and winked at him.

Raghav laughed, "This is the backbencher speaking!"

"Oh, those days! You used to give away your books from your home library to students on rent."

"Yeah! Technically, that was my first startup. I should change my PR."

Keshav smiled, as they both got nostalgic remembering their school days.

They chatted and drank for a couple of hours more and time flew by. A sinking feeling of leaving London and going back to Delhi had already started to overpower Raghav. He was slipping in his thoughts. Towards the end of a long trip to any good place, he always had this weird feeling of summer break coming to an end. The only good part about this journey back home was that he was returning with a new territory for his company and a giant client at hand. Not to miss, several good leads as well that would mature over a period of time. This gave him the rush of excitement that kept him going.

Raghav and Keshav hugged as they bid farewell. As Raghav almost turned around to leave, Keshav called out, "Raghav!" he said with a gleam and a wink, "You won't find the girl... if you stop looking for her!"

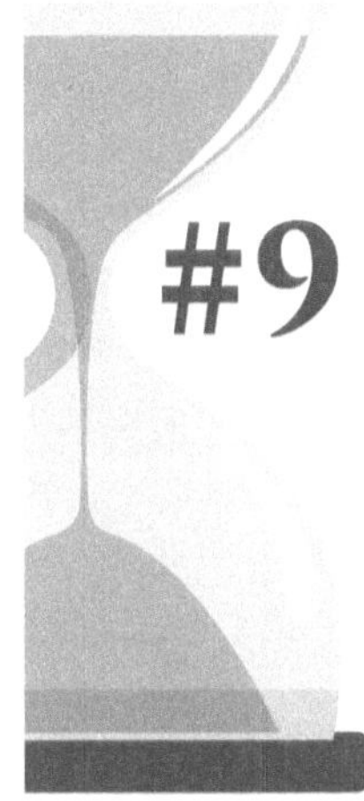

#9

Raghav scrolled through his social media feed as he waited for the boarding announcement at Heathrow Airport in London. He had checked in, bought stuff from the duty free stores, had a beer at the lounge, and still had 40 minutes remaining, before the boarding. Raghav loved airports and the atmospheric excitement of them. The rush, the sound of aircrafts, the expressions of travellers around and of course, the premium lounges!

Suddenly, his eyes stopped at an extremely opinionated and deeply analytical post on the political scenario of India and he got down to reading it. During the times when he was avoiding political judgements and debates on social media, this one was of particular interest. He read through it. Riya Bansal, he registered the name in his mind. The investigative skills of a millennial got to work and he checked out her profile and her work background. Being true to his entrepreneurial side, he opened her profile on LinkedIn in parallel.

He tried to recollect why they were friends on Facebook. Political volunteering, marketing, business development and currently expanding the family business, the profile intrigued Raghav. It struck him that they had very briefly met at an event some two years ago in Delhi, where he was a speaker. One of their mutual connections had introduced them and they had exchanged pleasantries.

Something pulled Raghav towards the profile. He had a fleeting feeling of butterflies in his stomach and a small chill down the spine of his neck. That something… made him smile.

He debated whether to message her or not. His ego clashed with his lonely self. He did not want to seem too eager and at the same time, his mind kept repeating the same arguments of lack of time and a lot of work pressure, all well-rehearsed thoughts he had been using to condition himself since his breakup. He decided to let it go. And suddenly, Keshav's words rang a bell in his mind – *"You won't find the girl…if you stop looking for her!"*

This gave him a sudden jerk, and instinctively he dropped Riya a message – "Hey! Long time!"

For the next few minutes, he waited and kept checking back his notifications like a teenager. But not for long. The boarding announcement and queuing up diverted him and like a pragmatic young snob, he forgot about it.

He found his seat, put his phone on flight mode, and dozed off, waiting to touch down on his own land in a couple of hours.

He slept like a tired baby, with no idea of what awaited him back in India.

* * *

Delhi's polluted air felt homelike. The peak traffic hour, the chaotic roads, the Metro going over the roads, and the everyday hustle of the common man – this was home. With a fresh feeling and a new vibe, he entered his Delhi office. Everyone broke into applause with the back wall of the seating area, proudly saying, 'Now in London.'

He greeted and hugged everyone as the entire team celebrated the new milestone. The Delhi team was fifteen people strong. Raghav hugged Disha and said, "Let us meet in my cabin with the core ones in 10 minutes."

Disha nodded and rounded up everyone as Raghav settled down in his cabin. He plugged in his laptop and on the whiteboard behind his chair, explained about the account of Creton Solutions and its deliveries to the core team. They all nodded, made notes, and grasped every bit of it.

"Guys, we have a week to crack this before we on-board them. Ideally, we were supposed to start today, but I received a message from their Product Head today that we have to push it further by a week due to some of their internal delays."

"That is good," said Farukh, "I think it is better that we have a week more with you being in office."

"Of course, Farukh. You guys are free to ask anything, any time of the day. Also, you lead the product and client delivery.

This project might need more people. Put out for hiring in your team, if the need be."

"Definitely. I will chalk out the requirement and analyse accordingly, Raghav. Don't worry," replied Farukh confidently.

"Our investors have some conversations going on for a further round of funding as well. So, I guess, hiring in advance won't be an issue," said Raghav, not so excited about the prospect.

"Were you not against raising more funds in the first place?" Disha asked immediately, looking straight into his eyes.

"Uh! I was. In fact, I still am. You guys have ESOPs, you all are my partners. You should know," Raghav thumped into his chair and continued, "We are under pressure from our investors. Plus, since they are confident on another round of funds they want us to slash our low-ticket clients and put more of our bandwidth on the big guys."

"Fuck! Raghav, you categorically said that the low paying clients were the backbone of the company because they gave us their accounts when we were nothing! Our entire concept was to make advertising reach every neighbourhood business owner in Tier II and III cities of India as well. And some of these guys have been with us for over two years now. Also, we have discussed this before – aren't these guys 35% of our business?" Disha argued frantically, throwing one fact after the other like bullet rounds.

"I know all of that, Disha! I know the numbers!" Raghav argued back, filled with irritation. "Investors think that we can fill in that gap of 35% with Creton for the time being. Also, they want us to focus our strengths on expanding more into the UK and in Europe as well. And they believe that continuing to deliver services to the small guys here would be an unnecessary drain on our limited resources."

"You call the shots, bro," Farukh pitched in, concerned but with belief in Raghav. "Personally, I strongly believe that it is too soon for us to eye further inroads into Europe. Creton and maybe a few more clients in the UK should be a good start for revenues and from there we can expand our footprints slowly and cautiously. Also, we have so much of a market to capture in India itself."

"Huh! It is weird that as a founder, I have to tell the investors that I don't want to raise money and that I want to go slow. Plus, that I want to retain the low-paying clients as well, even if they give us lower margins," Raghav massaged his temples with his hands to make his metaphorical headache feel better. "Anyway, right now is the time to work our asses off. Let me figure out these things. These things need deliberation."

Raghav concluded the meeting with his statement as everyone got to work. Over the next few days, new hiring took place, as Raghav painfully phased out seven of his low paying clients citing bandwidth issues. Some of them were ready to increase the retainer, but he cited several weird excuses, finally letting them go.

He picked up his phone to call one of his first clients ever.

"Raghav, how have you been?" Mr Shah asked joyfully

"All good, Sir. Had to travel a lot back and forth, so could not keep in touch. I hope the team was taking good care meanwhile," Raghav said apologetically. In his journey of creating this company, he had made sure that he talked personally with every client at least once a month or even more. Not only because he wanted to give that personal touch, but also because he loved this part of staying connected and creating these relationships.

"Of course! Disha and Farukh have been in constant touch, helping us in our new campaigns and sales funnels," said Mr Shah. He owned a jewellery brand in Jaipur. His tone changed a bit as he continued, "I received your mail about the phasing out of the contract and not doing it for another year. Is everything okay?"

His concern made Raghav sink further. "Yes sir, nothing to worry. It is just that we have been iterating on our model and working on some better features and analytics to serve clients in an improvised manner."

"But our relationship has been over two years now. See, if we can continue in the meantime on a revised contract with lesser deliverables. And if there is any issue, Raghav, a fund crunch or something, please tell me frankly. I will try my best to extend any help that I can."

Raghav sighed sadly. This was one of the earliest clients of VigyaPun and also one of the smallest in numbers. Obviously, as a business it took as much team bandwidth as a mid-segment client would take. But Raghav wanted to work with these businesses.

"Nothing like that, Sir. So honestly, we have investor pressure mounting or remodelling the business. Our focus areas are changing and we are pivoting on new models," Raghav tried to cover up as discreetly as he could.

Mr Shah remained quiet for a few seconds trying to comprehend the complex terminologies and making sense of the conversation.

Raghav continued, out of discomfort from the silence. "However, I would offer you three months of continued service and ensure that there is no hiccup in your marketing functions. Hopefully, in the meantime we would have figured out our solution and we will switch you to the new model as well!"

Mr Shah suddenly lightened up with a newfound zeal!

"That would be brilliant! I hope we continue working together. It is exciting to work with you guys. You have such a young and optimistic team. We have genuinely increased our business by almost 125-130% in the last few years with such targeted spends on marketing and advertising."

It felt like a blessing to Raghav. This is what he craved for. This is what made him proud of his company and his team. This is what he longed to hear every day at work! A sudden rush of gratitude filled him and without thinking of the consequences, he replied, "We are working 24 hours to give you the same experience, Sir. Your account will not be affected while we pivot more models. Thank You!"

He hung up with a huge smile on his face. He knew he could not replicate this answer to other older clients and he had to do away with them. He felt sad, as most of them had similar things to say and experiences to share. Businesses that had no awareness of technology and digital were benefiting from VigyaPun's advertising and targeting tools, blended with their creative custom campaigns. Digital Transformation of these businesses was the entire idea of setting up this company, in the first place. Raghav got back to his work, as he still had to decide on what to answer to the investors about retaining this client, and on the sad replies and excuses he had to make to other clients for letting them go.

❋ ❋ ❋

During the next few weeks, Raghav and Disha hung out a couple of times, catching up over beers in the evening or going out to cafes and working from there just to be quiet in their own zones. Their friendship had always been comfortable. They discussed work, but knew when to get it out of their systems. They understood each other and knew when to unwind. They had, both crazy nights with unending drinking sprees and quiet coffee evenings working on their laptops.

Raghav updated Disha about his London trip, his catch up with Keshav, also the short instance of checking out Riya Bansal on Facebook. He had not actively thought about Riya since that messaging incident at Heathrow, but at the same time, she had not left his mind. It was an incomprehensible space and he was almost afraid to sort out the mess in his mind.

"So, we are on for tonight, guys," Raghav excitedly asked the entire core team members, who worked on their laptops in a brainstorming meeting in his cabin. Farukh, Disha, Raghav,

Kriti, and Trisha were all very closely knit, as they had all been in the company, on an average, for over a year.

"I never miss your party, dude. You know that…" Farukh replied in an instant, almost ready already.

It was one of the regular parties at Raghav's bachelor pad. The dimmest light possible, chips, fries and bare minimum snacks and almost unlimited liquor were the regular features of Raghav's parties, which started not before 10 in the night and ended not before 5 in the morning. They used to do it almost every week and sometimes even more. While in Delhi, they all considered Raghav's house to be their own.

Soft music played as Farukh started a round of games involving everyone. They did not realise when the clock struck three, by which time Trisha and Disha had already passed out and slept on the sofa. Raghav stood in the balcony alone, his favourite spot in the house.

He was fairly high, happy in his normal thoughts about his life choices and future decisions, as he smoked looking at the expanse of empty land right beside his tower.

"Planning to buy that whole piece of land and build a new office?" said Farukh, referring to the land that Raghav was staring at, as he joined him in the balcony and sat in the rocking chair that Raghav had lovingly purchased online to spend time reading on wintery Sunday afternoons. He did not get time to do that very often, but the chair was a much loved spot for people who came to party at his place.

"Ha! I wish!" said Raghav, smirking, "Just thinking about the regular stuff that I often do!"

"All is well, Raghav. You worry too much. You are a successful 28-year-old entrepreneur! People love you."

"But that is not all that it takes. The responsibility of running a company, and maintaining the trust that people put in you is a constant reminder of the things that maybe I am not grateful for. Kicking out our low paying clients was a very tough decision. I haven't been able to take my mind off it!"

"I understand. But that is again because you are a good person. I often think where life would take us. Life gives weird choices, makes you stand at crossroads that you cannot comprehend sometimes..." said Farukh, getting up from the chair and standing against the balcony railing. Raghav looked at him, suddenly baffled with the flow of wisdom from Farukh, which was a bit uncharacteristic of him. He was a man of few words who always talked sense and only as much required.

"Umm... right. But crossroads are good, as long as both paths lead you to a better life. Comparing between two good paths is a lucky choice that life gives!"

"Yes, absolutely. It is a 'good' problem to have. But then, choosing one path might put all your relations, your work, your respect at stake while promising you successes that you cannot imagine!" said Farukh, deep in his thoughts.

"If your relations, work, and respect are at stake, I wonder what success would that path offer?" Raghav asked him, looking back at his life and the decisions that he made. He had always put relationships first in his dealings, may it be his colleagues or his clients. Sometimes this attitude led him into loss making deals or deals that did not make any sense to investors, but Raghav wanted to work. He wanted to work and build a company while creating ever-lasting relationships. He often said 'People should remember our company name for the relationship that they had with us.'

"Not everyone is privileged, Raghav. Money is a parameter of success for many… probably, most!"

"I agree with you. It is for me, as well. But would such money be digestible? Money that puts everything dear to you at stake? Basically, it is a question of what drives you, Farukh. There is no problem in money being the driving factor."

"The answer that everyone seeks, but yet most do not find!" Disha interrupted the conversation with a drunken wisdom thrown at both of them suddenly.

They both laughed. "So, the devil is up again?" Farukh teased Disha.

"Of course! Your boring conversations about the wisdom of life haunted me in my dreams. I had to wake up and start another round of drinks to be able to drown in the sorrows of choosing between the crossroads!"

They all laughed as Disha increased the volume of music and Farukh filled all their glasses. It was the second innings of a night that was full of laughter and craziness.

#10

Raghav sat in his cabin, working on Creton's account research, and planning on further expansion into the European markets. No major breakthrough had come through after Creton and it frustrated Raghav, as he did not want his London trip to be termed as a waste. He continuously followed up with the people he had met and tried to set up further calls and presentations. To justify the expenses calculated of their new plan for the expansion, Raghav wanted at least three to four clients of Creton's magnitude.

He was scrolling through his excel sheet with the lead statuses, when a new mail popped up—from Farukh. He looked through the cabin's glass and realised Farukh was not in the office. He imagined the reason was a hangover from last night's party.

The mail staggered Raghav. Farukh had sent in his resignation, a mix of guilt and gratitude. Farukh had written how working with Raghav and VigyaPun was a learning experience beyond words, but at the same time, how he had higher aspirations and wanted a big leap in his career. He had been offered a Co-Founder position in his childhood friend's startup, with equal fifty per cent equity. The startup had recently raised funding and wanted Farukh on board as co-founder and the Head of Technology.

Raghav immediately called Disha to his cabin and told her everything. She read the mail, and covered her face with her hands.

"Traitor!" exclaimed Disha.

"Disha! You are being harsh…" Raghav said calmly, scrolling through his mobile.

"Raghav, how can you possibly be so calm after this? He led our entire Tech. How are we going to work through Creton?"

"I have dropped a message to some of my industry friends for finding us a replacement ASAP. Please update Twinkle as well; her HR skills are needed at best right now."

"I will do that. I will also spread the word in my network, but how could he, Raghav?"

"I have no clue. Maybe I understand some of his vague conversations from last night, now."

"Whatever be the reason, Raghav. He had always been in the most confidential discussions. He had ESOPs and ownership in the company. He gave all of this up for a bloody co-founder tag in a new startup!"

"That happens, Disha. You need to calm down. I am shocked as well, but maybe it was for the best. He must have thought of the pros and cons," said Raghav, with Farukh's mail still open on his laptop.

"Why can't people in our generation stick their ass to one company and grow with it? Few more thousands, a stupid tag of a designation and their loyalties shake!"

Raghav smiled sadly. "That is the truth, Disha. But I would say, a bit insensitive. Money is a driving factor in fact. That is what Farukh and I talked about last night!"

"Yes, but wouldn't it be bigger money and better position in the long run, if they stick with one company. VigyaPun gave him a name and standing in the Industry. He was invited to conferences. He represented our company so many times. This is just so sad! People are not able to have a longer-term vision at all. Quick money and easy success is what everyone is aspiring for."

"Let it be, Disha. All we can do is wish him the best going forward. Finding his replacement and bringing them to this level will be a task in itself."

"True, a lot of training and effort will go into it from scratch!"

"Yeah, thankfully we have a bigger team now who can guide the new person on SOPs, and both of us can spend some more time on honing this new person."

"Of course, Raghav. Let us move beyond this and see what else we have in store for ourselves! This company is going to give me a very high blood pressure some day and the blame will be on you," Disha shook her head.

"Thanks for the very kind words! And Disha…" said Raghav, as she stood up to leave the cabin. "Let us keep this between us right now. A core team member leaving the company suddenly doesn't send a good message for a lean team startup like ours!"

Raghav pulled his chair back in and closed his eyes contemplating.

It was one of the quiet evenings at Raghav's bachelor pad. Raghav was relishing and appreciating his self-cooked meal, while watching a web series. Disha had just updated him that the final on boarding of Creton could start any minute now, as the backend was ready and she was leaving the office now.

His phone beeped; the time was 11 pm and as a happy surprise, the notification showed 'Riya Bansal'. He sprang up in excitement and opened his chat box.

"I am so sorry for replying to you this late. I had been really busy and stuck up with a few new initiatives at work. Glad to get connected with you again."

Raghav read it a few times and without sounding too eager, treaded carefully. "That is great. Just thought of catching up on how has life been?"

"It has been treating me fine! I follow your updates often. You are truly a 'startup guy', ahan!"

"Don't really appreciate that tag. But maybe, yes, a tag that I cannot run away from!"

"What is wrong about being identified as a startup guy?"

"Haha! Nothing really. Being a startup guy comes with its own challenges and sacrifices."

"Ooooh! A heavy one, indeed. Sacrifices are a part of moving ahead, otherwise what you really want will be sacrificed! The choice is yours…"

"Spoken like a true businesswoman!"

The chat continued for half an hour more without a break. Raghav had never been into chatting coherently like this. He loved the conversation and the whole vibe of it. There was a certain spark that you rarely feel in digital conversations. Or maybe, it was just Raghav and his hidden loneliness.

Raghav had convinced himself superficially that a relationship was not meant for him at the moment. However, despite his office parties and hanging out, he felt a void deep inside him. Every day when he returned to his home after the day's work, he felt this weird need to share his emotions with someone. The human need for a meaningful conversation and support. He wanted to share his success and challenges, his good days and the bad ones with someone and wanted his partner to do the same with him.

He was a sensitive person inside, which he had successfully hidden and dominated it with an aggressive entrepreneurial streak. The fast-paced startup journey, with ups and downs multiple times in a single day had subdued the emotions inside him. He did party with his team very often with loud music, crazy shots and junk food, but his heart metaphorically longed for a quaint balcony evening with wine and a partner, to share long conversations. The loud music drowned this feeling deep somewhere.

As his mind thought about all this, he felt a sudden emptiness cropping in. Was his mental health deteriorating? He feared. He thought about the hundreds of first generation entrepreneurs who like him struggled every day to run a company, and all that they sacrificed. It was hard to comprehend this feeling of silence inside him despite the growth of his company and the laughter he shared with people in his office. It was as if experiencing a dual life, as if he was thinking about two different people.

Even as these thoughts raced in his mind, with desperation and desolation, he continued chatting with Riya, in the best of his moods. His dual thoughts scared him in a weird way. Away from his loving family, broken up from a long relationship and separated from his childhood friends due to the shackles of work and distance, he was alone.

In a 2 BHK plush apartment, he felt small. He felt unimportant and insignificant. Would he be able to make out of this ever? Would he ever find someone who could share his emotions and hold his hand? He put his thoughts together. Even at the slightest hint of such thoughts, he often immersed himself into work as self-defence. He frantically continued to chat with Riya.

"Got to finish off some errands before I hit the bed…" Riya replied, inching towards ending the conversation. This could be a dead end, like most first-conversations around the world. Raghav realised he had to do something quick.

"Of course! How about catching up some time soon?"

"I wouldn't mind. Are you in a hurry or something?"

"Uh! Not at all…"

"Here is my number, in case you want to move out of social media and talk sometime," Riya replied. Raghav mentally high-fived himself.

"I am catching a flight to Kolkata tomorrow though. Going for work, so I might be busy for a few days."

Something twisted inside Raghav and without second thought, he typed back, "What a coincidence! I am flying out to Jaipur tomorrow… Let us catch up at the airport?"

As soon as he read his own message after sending, he felt desperate. Why did he even do that? Will he even get a reply after this?

He saw Riya typing. Moments passed by like ages.

"Wow! That is truly a coincidence. Let us coordinate and meet at Terminal 3 tomorrow then?"

Raghav smiled and lay down to sleep with the best thoughts in his mind. Since Farukh's leaving, this was the first time he had felt positive in days. He felt good about talking to someone new. He felt fresh and uplifted, as he put his phone aside and stared at the ceiling thinking about the conversation and replaying it in his mind.

Suddenly, his phone beeped with a new Skype message. He paused his thoughts for a moment, as he knew Skype these days was generally Craig Skelton himself. While the rest of his team communicated with Raghav on WhatsApp, Craig was one of those 'professional' ones who did not use WhatsApp much.

Raghav swiped his phone open and read the message from Craig Skelton –

"Hello Raghav. Trust you are doing good.

I feel extremely bad about conveying this, but facing huge troubles. The last push of seven days was because of some internal discussions about outsourcing. Recession hit us hard and the board is not approving any outsourcing for advertising and lead management at the moment. We have to hold off on the project for now. I know it is highly unprofessional and it is very embarrassing for me after our entire discussion, but it's kind of a Force Majeure at the moment.

Stay in touch.
Hoping to associate with you on something very soon.

Regards."

Raghav read the message seven to eight times. Numb, he dropped his phone on the bed.

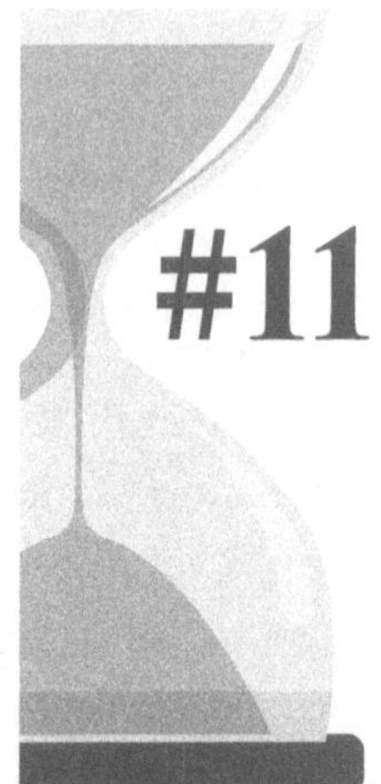

#11

It was past midnight. Raghav sat beside the toilet seat, completely drained out after vomiting a couple of times. He had pangs of anxiety as his stomach churned. Thousands of things sprang up in quick succession in his mind; every minute, at such a fast paced rate that he felt he may have a breakdown. He tried hard to compose himself several times, but his heartbeat raced faster than ever.

Completely unrelated events raced through his mind in audio-visual sequence. At one moment, he was in a cafe breaking up with Kanika, as he said – *"It is a 10 million USD valued, investor funded company, Kanika,"* and the next minute he was on the Jubilee Line of the London Tube reading an article about the thriving advertising sector in the UK. Keshav's awe of his startup, Disha's undying belief in him, his parents' reaction to leaving a well-paying consulting job – everything flashed through his brain like a soap opera, as he vomited again.

He felt dizzy. He was shaking. He was scared.

He felt a weird vacuum again, an awkward fear from being alone in the house. Senseless and scary calculations raced through his mind – like how much time would it take for someone to find out he was dead in the house. Probably, not before the maid arrived at 8 the next morning.

Riya Bansal's entire Facebook profile ran past his eyes, for no reason whatsoever. He suddenly decided to bring himself together. He mustered whatever strength he had and stood up with the support of the washbasin. He looked into the mirror at his reflection. He stared into his own dead empty eyes. It did not help, as he felt more frightened, and lonelier than ever.

He did not know whom to call or whom to reach out to. Instinctively, he washed his face. He washed his face several times as if it would wash down his worries and undo the Skype message of Craig.

Fuck! The word echoed in his mind. Hundreds of scenarios ran wild. He had let go of low paying clients already under pressure and extended offer letters for three new senior-level positions. Expenses mounted, as revenues had just tanked suddenly.

Funding—he remembered that the investors had some funding options almost finalised. That would be a splendid breather right now. But, those funding options were not signed yet, and nothing in the startup world is more fleeting than a funding option until it is signed.

Suddenly, he realised how lonely he was. Despite the hundreds of people who thronged his sessions in conferences and thousands of college students who attended his motivational talks, he was alone.

He kept washing his face until his skin felt raw. He felt empty inside, probably because he had vomited a lot. He could not think. His mind could not function. He just unlocked his phone and dialled a number, almost unknowingly.

"Raghav, it's quite late. Is everything okay?" Naina, one of Raghav's acquaintances and his psychologist for a very brief period, said in a very sleepy voice.

"Naina, I lost one of the biggest deals of my life. My entire plan of expanding into the UK is down the drain. I sacrificed a lot of things professionally and personally for this expansion plan, even took decisions against my will and ethics," said Raghav, without a pause, still panting from the vomiting.

Naina being a well-wisher and a psychologist sensed the situation within seconds. "Raghav, calm down. Take a deep breath. We will talk it out. But first you need to find composure."

"Naina, you don't understand. I have salaries to pay and investors to be satisfied. I can't afford to fail, Naina. What will Riya think?"

"I know everything, Raghav. I understand and…uh, wait… who is Riya?"

"Uh! What should I do, Naina?"

"Okay, Raghav. First of all, this is not the end of the world. Being an entrepreneur, you should understand this more than anyone else. I always tell you that you don't have to think of the worst case scenario. There must be a hundred other ways of fighting the situation and coming out of it triumphant."

Raghav listened intently, but could not come up with any reply other than a meek 'hmm'.

"Raghav, you have to clear your head and sleep. Otherwise, it will result in a breakdown and you won't be able to find the right solutions in time for the challenges you face. Your mind needs rest. Do you want to wake up in the morning, go to your office, and fight this goddamn situation?"

"Yes!"

"Good, then you need to lie down. Tell me you are on your bed and trying to sleep?"

Raghav walked towards the bed almost limping and fell on the bed with a thud.

"You have to do a lot of things, Raghav. You have to mend things and work for others. That is what you do, and that is what you are passionate about. I won't ask you to come and visit me tomorrow, but give me a call if you feel like, once you have rested and you are in office," Naina said in a very calm voice. It did not seem as if she was pissed off from being woken up in the middle of the night.

"Naina, what do you think of me and the decisions that I have taken in the last few years?"

"Raghav, not as a psychologist, but as someone who has known you and seen your journey, I want to tell you this," said Naina, continuing in her placid demeanour, "You are one of the strongest people I have ever met. You inspire me to take difficult decisions and then make them right. Success and failure are a part of life. If life doesn't give you both, then you are living an extremely linear life. It might be a weak moment, Raghav. But let me tell you this, you will bounce out of it."

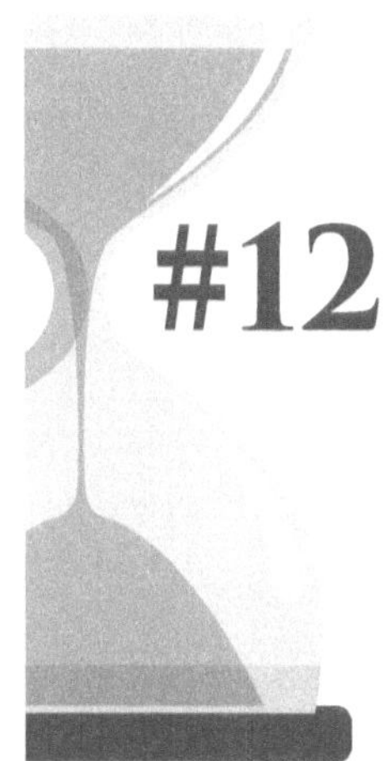

#12

The bright sunlight bounced off Raghav's face and he woke up, feeling dreary and exhausted. He had forgotten to draw the curtains last night. *Craig Skelton.* The name rang bells in his mind. He did not feel outraged or angry about it. He just felt numb. It was an unexplainable feeling.

Not even a particle of his body wanted to get out of the bed and start the day. The mere thought of his team working their asses off on something that was not happening anymore, was disheartening. He shifted uncomfortably and finally pushed himself out of his bed. After a quick customary bath, lasting a few minutes, he rushed to his office, feeling demotivated and under confident.

He greeted everyone cheerlessly, as he entered and gave his usual line of morning instructions, while walking to his cabin. "Tarak, please get me yesterday's client delivery report. Jagriti, update me on yesterday's outstanding report. Disha, need some changes to the offering side. Let us sit whenever you are free."

He moved to his cabin slyly. He felt a weird guilt, as if someone would know if he looked them in the eyes.

Disha entered the cabin only after a few seconds and said, "What happened?"

"Um. As in? W… What happened?" he said, trying to cover it up with a fake surprise.

"Not a single smile, no high-fives and most importantly, not a single swear word since you have entered the office!"

Raghav looked at her with a dead look. "Creton pulled out. They are not going to work with us due to some financial troubles and board mandate."

Disha dropped dead in the nearest chair. She could not comprehend what to say. She understood in a second about what was at stake here.

"I have a call scheduled with the board in 5 minutes, Disha. Sorry but you will have to leave the cabin to me. I will fill you in as soon as I have any update on what is going to happen. I have informed the board about it and they are discussing this with potential investors right now and getting us funding confirmations."

"Yes…of course! I understand. Buzz me when you need me," said Disha and walked towards the door. "Raghav, whatever happens, we are in this together."

Raghav gave her a meek smile in response.

He revolved his chair and looked outside the window behind his table. The fast moving traffic helped Raghav get lost in the rush. He stared outside as he lost the track of time and space. He leaned back and closed his eyes.

His phone rang with a jarring noise. It was a calendar reminder for the call with the board. He was 10 minutes late already. He joined the conference call immediately.

"... not something we can help..." one of the investors was animatedly speaking, when he joined it.

Pradeep immediately cut in, "So gentlemen, we have Raghav with us. As we all know, it is an extremely crucial call, which shall hopefully end in some very critical decisions. Before we begin, or anyone gives any update, I want to make it clear, Raghav; none of us are blaming you. You are an entrepreneur and so are we. Such things happen in businesses very often and are outside our control."

"Yes sir. Of course," replied Raghav, mentally thanking Pradeep.

"So, I have an update, guys," said a board member, who had been most actively looking for funding. Raghav's senses lit up at his voice. "Obviously, potential investors had to be told that UK business looks blurry right now with the new situation. We can't keep them in the dark."

Everyone agreed in tandem, as he continued, "I spoke with almost everyone on our radar in the last one and a half hours, and it seems we have almost no, or at best very bleak hope of raising funds in the current scenario."

Raghav punched his fist on the table and mouthed, 'Fuck' silently, trying to maintain his calm gulping down a glass of water.

"Most of them believe that this is an ad-tech business, which is anyway going to see a lot of negative graphs as recession sets in and budgets will plummet. We have a very weak service and creative side of the model, and most of our business depends on technology. It is hard to show investors any recurring, stable business opportunity."

Everyone fell silent. No one had any option left. The worst thing Raghav had been dreading all this while was then spoken by another board member, who had otherwise been quiet, "I think I would like to officially exit at this stage. Funding and businesses are going down everywhere, and even we need to maintain our liquidity."

Other board members agreed with him immediately, as if they had just been waiting for someone to bring it up.

"Sirs please. Ad-Tech is an extremely huge business opportunity. For the time being, we can focus on the Indian market and penetrate further. So many businesses need affordable branding and creative services also. We can expand into that..." Raghav frantically said whatever came to his mind.

"Raghav, Raghav... You are not a service company. You have never pitched as one. You do not have a creative team on board. We cannot hire at this stage and the revenues have taken a deep hit."

For the next fifteen to twenty minutes, everyone discussed prospects and genuine options to do something to keep the company afloat. There were none. Funding scenario in the country was drying up very fast, as even bigger unicorns had fallen recently. Current investors did not want to invest further and dig deeper, technology was no longer an attraction for people and everyone was focussed on 'real' business. The low barriers to entry in the sector and the global markets closing up, things looked extremely bad.

"Sir, you said, funding would be the best option at this stage…"

"Raghav, we had all said a lot of things with the assumption that Creton would be on board."

"You cannot decide to leave the company at this stage, Sir," Raghav said in a low tone, almost sad.

"Raghav, even if we stay and do not get anything out of it, it means nothing, except added legal hassles for us in future," a board member said curtly.

"Pradeep Sir?" said Raghav, as if his last hope was still alive.

"Raghav…" said Pradeep after listening to everyone and a lot of deliberation. " Unfortunately, I agree with all the gentlemen here and the picture looks bleak to me as well.

Raghav thumped his head on the table and looked down.

"However… The only support I can think of right now,"

Pradeep continued slowly, as if weighing his every word. "... is Ritesh Lalwani."

"Ritesh Lalwani?" Raghav asked, trying to connect. He had known this name.

"The Bollywood producer?" one of the board members asked incredulously.

"Uh yes. Ritesh was a good friend before he became one of the leading producers in Bollywood, and we are fellow members of a business organisation. I haven't been in touch for a few years, but he is very kind. He will not refuse a meeting."

It suddenly struck Raghav like a bolt. "He has recently launched his own Media Incubator and Fund!"

"Correct! I will drop him a text and set up a meeting for you. Can you travel to Mumbai next week?"

"Anywhere sir! Anywhere!" Raghav exclaimed, with a new wave of hope and excitement.

#13

"Welcome to Chhatrapati Shivaji International Airport, Mumbai. Proud to announce yet another before-time landing…"

Raghav woke up with a start to the screech of the touchdown and the monotonous welcome message of the cabin crew. In no time, he collected his baggage and proceeded to the cab pickup point. The heavy coastal breeze and the feel of Mumbai hit him in the face, as soon as he stepped out of the airport. It was a brief one-night stay in Mumbai. The early morning flight had already messed with his sleep, and he had a meeting in three hours. He had chosen a hotel closer to Ritesh's office in Lower Parel to save commute time.

Mumbai was as busy as ever. Overcrowded roads, overpowering hoardings and overwhelming skyscrapers made Mumbai truly and in the most clichéd ways, the city of dreams. The traffic was already starting to suffocate even at

7.30 in the morning and the roadside food vendors had already made a good sale.

He checked into his hotel, took a quick shower, and changed into his formals. He reached Ritesh's office building 30 minutes in advance and decided to finally grab a quick bite, at the nearest vada pav vendor. Tall buildings surrounded the landscape stylishly. Mumbai had a charm of its own. The truly cosmopolitan charm, apparently.

Finally, he decided to walk into the plush, 30-storey building, straight after eating a delicious vada pav.

"I have a meeting scheduled with Mr Ritesh Lalwani at 11.30 am," he told the receptionist.

"Yes Mr Raghav. Ritesh's assistant Chandan will shortly guide you to the Conference Room D."

Raghav sat in the waiting area surrounded with life size wallpapers of upcoming Bollywood movies. He could see a team of sixty to seventy people seated through a glass wall, deeply engrossed in their work, without much interaction with each other.

Two huge LED screens were on the wall across the hall, showing the real-time Google trends and Twitter trends on the on-going movie promotions.

A tall man walked from a distance towards him and greeted him with a smile. Chandan was Ritesh's assistant for twenty-three years now. Raghav tried to make his best impression and quick small talk, while he was escorted towards a conference room. Raghav checked his messages once before entering the room, as he knew he would be busy for the next few hours.

Except for the regular work messages and office group chats, he had a message from Pradeep. "Had a quick call with the board again today, Raghav. This meeting seems to be your very last chance. No pressure, but crack it, else we all go down together."

No pressure! Raghav read again in his mind and smirked. A message so pressurizing in itself ironically said 'No pressure'. This was classic Pradeep Kapoor.

He entered the conference room, almost shaking. He wanted to smoke badly and drank an entire glass of water in anxiety. It was one of those moments when you want to have water and pee badly at the same time. He seated himself and connected his laptop to the projector as Chandan had instructed.

Few seconds later, Ritesh entered the conference room.

"Hello Ritesh, I am Raghav."

"Hello Raghav, pleasure meeting you. Shall we start?" said Ritesh, clearly not much into pleasantries and weather conversations. He was a sharp-witted man, uptight and spectacled as an add-on to his extremely serious demeanour.

"Of course!"

Raghav switched on his presentation and began with the entire journey of VigyaPun, the pride in his voice coming to him naturally and bringing with it the confidence he desperately needed. His story and the growth of VigyaPun was not the difficult part to explain, as the numbers said it all. However, explaining the difficult times of the last six to seven months was the tricky part. The funding drying up, the ecosystem going weak and the economy not being favourable for young businesses and startups were not good enough excuses for an investor.

He gave his best shot and showed all the bright sides of VigyaPun hoping that his passion will make up for any shortcomings. As for his expansion plans, he reiterated the story of expanding into Europe and the UK, as had been discussed with his existing investors.

Raghav felt the meeting went off well. He ended with the funding requirement of $1 Million for an immediate roadmap of ten to twelve months. He was prepared for the worst even in case of an approval – that he would become a minority shareholder now in his own company. With limited options to survive, this was the worst that could happen. *Wait second to worst. Worst would be closing down, if this funding didn't come through.* He thought to himself.

The lights came on again in the room and Raghav looked at Ritesh and tried to read his expression. Ritesh was thinking something, still looking at the screen on the wall with the last slide of the funding requirement.

"Hmm…" said Ritesh and took a deep breath.

Raghav's anxiety rose with every passing second.

"Okay Raghav, so tell me honestly, how do you see Ad-Tech growing further, especially in the current times? Do you really think technology is all that it takes to survive?"

"Um, no Ritesh. Technology is not the only thing we thrive on. It's an integrated service model…"

"With no barrier to entry! Considering that there is no creative touch to your offering, your product is something that might get overpowered any day by all the digital media channels opening up their APIs, which they are doing already."

Raghav was intrigued with Ritesh's updated knowledge on both Ad-Tech and technology in general. He was impressed.

"Sir, we are constantly upgrading our service models as well, to have more and more retainer and long term business."

"Fair enough…"

Ritesh thought for another minute. "Your funding requirement is not a problem. Of course, Pradeep's recommendation adds a lot to it. I can even offer $2 million to give you a breathing space of another year to grow and scale up."

"Uh… okay…" Raghav was excited. Spellbound to be exact! He did not know how to react.

"There would be a few terms. Chandan will give you more details."

"Sure Ritesh. Thanks a lot."

"Glad to meet you, Raghav," said Ritesh and straightaway walked out of the conference room in a jiffy.

Raghav sat on the chair, took a few deep breaths, and felt the adrenaline rush. He had already thought of the terms and was prepared to hear that he would not be the majority shareholder any more now. Draconian terms awaited him, he anticipated. Keeping the company afloat and not letting any of his team members lose their jobs was his utmost priority. He could go to any lengths of accepting the vulture-like terms of the deal for this.

He looked at the overwhelming Mumbai skyline through the glass wall of the conference room and watched cars and buses rush by, far down in the street.

Chandan walked into the room again with a few papers.

"So Raghav, there is something we need to discuss..."

"Of course, Chandan..." Raghav began to talk, showing that he was already prepared, only to be cut off by Chandan again.

"... which should remain within this conference room by all means."

Raghav raised an eyebrow, feeling awkward, but nodded.

"Ritesh agrees to the $2 million deal, but he has a condition."

"... which is?" asked Raghav, wanting Chandan to hurry with his conditions and get this done with, as he had mentally prepared himself to agree to the worst. It was about saving his goddamn company—saving his dream from crumbling down. He felt irritated with Chandan's slow speed, as if he was watching every word of his. *He has no idea that I am in no position of a negotiation. Take my approval, and get it done with!* Raghav thought to himself.

"You will have to spend some 'personal' time with Ritesh, if you know what I mean…spend some time with him privately. You have been invited to his place for dinner, tonight…Do you fully agree to that with your consent?"

Raghav looked dead into Chandan's eyes for a few seconds. Those were the slowest seconds of his life, with a deep sinking feeling. He picked up his laptop and walked out of the room straight towards the elevator.

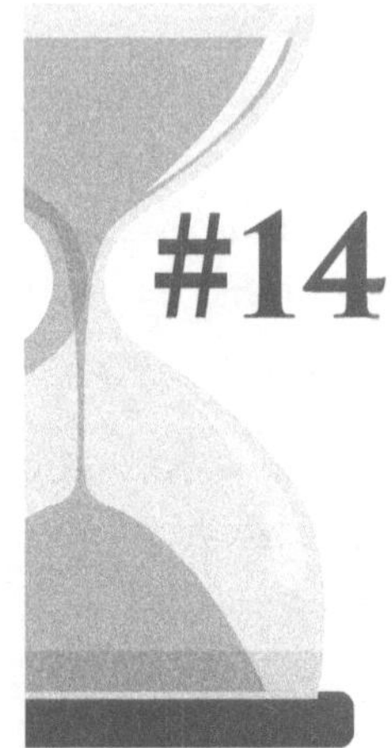

#14

Raghav sat in the farthest corner of Blue Tokai Cafe in the hustling area of Champa Gali, in the posh and upmarket South of Delhi. It was comparatively closer to his house in Faridabad, and Riya often came to South Delhi for her meetings and work. He checked his watch, as he eagerly waited for Riya.

After what happened in Mumbai, Raghav had been into his cocoon for some time. He decided to take things slow, one at a time and not hurry into a decision. However, he did realise that with every passing day his difficulties were rising. The smaller clients that they had done away with had already found some alternative and new clients would take a lot of time to bring on-board. Meanwhile, the expenses remained the same.

New hiring was immediately halted, but Raghav did not want even a single person from his old existing team to be fired. He revved up his efforts on business development from the existing strong geographies of Jaipur and New Delhi.

The business scenario was difficult as the entire world plunged into recession with difficult economic conditions. While the bigger robust business conglomerates survived and sailed through, the young entrepreneurs and startups faced the brunt.

People were wary of investing in marketing and advertising solutions, at a time when business continuity itself was difficult. Startups surviving only on funds started plummeting rapidly and so did numerous me-too models, which tried to copy other successful startups. Technology and Innovation were not the highlight keywords any more, but only 'Business' and 'Revenues' mattered.

At such a time, business acquisition was proving to be a challenge. The technology that VigyaPun had integrated, leaving behind their core creative angle years ago was now backfiring. Technology costs were difficult to sustain, including both the servers as well as the human resources. Smaller clients needed more of the human touch and creativity than technology alone. Operating with high Tech costs at this stage would be difficult.

Even during this fiasco, investors refused to support further and did not even let Raghav take out the technology from VigyaPun. It would mean a huge cost saving, but for investors that was the only 'USP' that kept the company attractive for any 'potential' investment. However, to Raghav, investments seemed to be a distant dream. The technology angle and the costs that came with it were proving to be the slow killer for the company as it bled inside.

Since Creton Solutions had pulled out and Raghav had suffered a massive anxiety attack, he had been in touch with Naina on and off, for advice on his mental stability. However, with Riya by his side and their constant meetings and conversations, Raghav felt amazing. She was the perfect mix of intellect, smartness, and maturity that Raghav had always looked for.

They often discussed their challenges and stories, and it felt as if facing all the problems together. Raghav told her everything that had been going on with VigyaPun and she had taken it without being judgemental or biased.

They shared a great rapport together. Raghav loved how Riya understood his emotions, his conversations, and even the moments when they were silent.

Riya took her seat opposite him. "You couldn't have found a more secluded corner here!"

"Just want to be away from the crowd. I don't feel like looking at people. Somehow, it feels as if they are all judging me and laughing at my failures!" Raghav said sadly.

"Oh come on, Raghav! Not being insensitive, but you need to come out of this pity party."

"Of course, you would say so! You don't know how it feels to be on this side of the spectrum," said Raghav, without realising and immediately regretted his remark.

"Everyone has a story, Raghav. And to bring you out of your self-centred world, no one really cares about yours. Everyone has their own problems and challenges. Be real! You are the smartest and most practical person I have ever met; you cannot let yourself down because of this."

Her words pierced Raghav because he knew she was right. But the words did not make him feel better.

"Forget it! Tell me about your on-going deal with the Gurgaon based company?" asked Raghav, trying to change the topic.

"Well, it bombed! We wanted to make the sale, but they had a vastly different price expectation. I am trying to expand my family's business in new verticals. The business name, the credentials and background doesn't help. These are young companies and startups that I am trying to deal with. It is a different ball game altogether."

"You have cracked some big accounts. I am sure you will get through more! You have the resources on your side."

"Working with a traditional setup has its own challenges. I have to bring on new business for my vertical and balance it with the orthodox and traditional working environment at my factory unit. Every day is a challenge trying to fight the numerous taboos. Plus, being a woman working in a traditional industry does not help at all."

"Then why take the pain of this entire new innovative vertical at all? Why did you not want to continue with what your family has always been doing?"

"I was always interested in the clothing line. I did not want to launch my own clichéd label, because it is already overdone and the fashion retail is extremely cluttered. Plus, my competence is in operations and business. I am not a design person. Also, the existing line of work is very streamlined and traditional. I want to create my own name in the industry and provide the easiest, most affordable solution to customised corporate clothing."

"Interesting. I never thought of it like that. At least, I am glad you have a clear vision and you know how to crack it. I am stuck at this weird dead end, where all my paths and options are closed!"

"Honestly, you know what?"

"Yeah?"

"You have told me your entire journey. It is impressive – I mean, the kind of work that you have done and the vision you had. I see how passionately you talk about creative advertising campaigns and the ideas you have. But don't you think you rushed into raising funds too soon?"

"In my defence, that was the need of the hour," said Raghav. He contemplated for a few seconds and then added, "Also, maybe I read and dived too deep into the 'startup' ecosystem and got swayed by the school of thought that funding is the only way to scale."

"Your investors are not letting go of the technology aspect from a creative business, thus creating a roadblock for you!"

"I know! I wanted to focus on the Tier II and III of the country. But with their backing and regular day-to-day monitoring, the vision kind of shifted to global expansion and creating a tech enabled solution to advertising."

"What are your options right now? I am here with you and I am sure we will figure out a way!" said Riya and softly placed her hand on Raghav's palm.

Raghav felt an unknown electricity. The softness of her hands and the assurance that she placed it with was beautiful. Raghav felt a vibe of being secure. His mental space where he had felt extremely void, now felt complete. He had not thought about falling into a relationship anymore some months ago, but he realised that the phases of life are abrupt and unexpected. He remembered what Keshav had told him in London. You won't find the girl… if you stop looking for her.

Amidst everything that was happening with VigyaPun right now, this was his safe place to be. The only place where he did not feel like a loser. The only place which uplifted him.

He pulled himself together and tightened his hand around Riya's. They looked deep into each other's eyes with faint smiles on their face. They read everything written there and remained silent for a few long minutes. This was the silence of reassurance of being there for each other. It felt like the start of something new.

"Uh!" Raghav sighed and shook his head trying to return to the real world and the on-going conversation. "All my options seem closed. The funding bubble of the startup ecosystem is bursting gradually, and the storm is taking away everything that I have built. Giving up my vision and aligning it to that of prospective investors was definitely a mistake…"

"No, it was a learning experience!" Riya interrupted. "You are young, Raghav. You have everything on your side. You have a great team, a great vision, a brilliant mind… You can start fresh!"

"Ha!" Raghav laughed mockingly. "Starting fresh? After this nightmare? I have not even thought about ending this yet, and you are talking about starting again?"

"I don't mean it like that. May it be inside this company or outside…"

"Existing investors will not let me start anything as of now. They think they have burnt their hands and are extremely wary of continuing anyway. It is all going down and I need to face this reality, which stares blankly in my eyes. Moreover, the team that you talk about! It has gained nothing being in this company. I will have to ensure that, they are all placed well enough, before we sink. That is my priority right now. It gives me sleepless nights, thinking about the aspirations and expectations they had from us!"

"I completely understand your situation. Anything I say would be unfair and undermining to this situation.

Raghav pushed back in his chair and covered his face in his palms. Riya looked at him concerned and serious.

"I need a break!" Raghav said frustrated. "Let us get drunk!"

Riya looked at him flabbergasted. "Are you the man who was whining about the current life situation seconds ago?"

"So? How does that stop someone from drinking down the

sorrows?" said Raghav, trying to smile.

"How eccentric are you!" Riya exclaimed. "But, I am on for it, of course! Social is nearby."

"Uh, no! Can you manage a night-out? Let us go to my place, have a few people over and party the shit out of this situation! If we are going down, let us make it memorable."

Riya shook her head in disbelief. She was intrigued with Raghav's entrepreneurial mind, and his mood swings. Surprisingly, she did not get upset or confused with his behaviour and mental switches. She went with the flow and enjoyed every bit of being in his company. This was the first time she was dating an entrepreneur. Her previous experiences had bombed and never lasted longer than a few days. She was too independent and smart to be led into a mundane relationship.

But this was different. She felt as if Raghav was a flowing river, pulling her with a strong current. She loved every bit of this. His idiosyncrasies intrigued her weirdly and she could not understand the magnetic energy in this relationship. She could never get enough of this.

What went on in Raghav's mind was incomprehensible and thus, it was like an adventurous ride for Riya every moment.

Disha, Kriti, Riya, and Raghav sat around the centre table in Raghav's lounge at his home. It was late evening and old school retro music created an atmosphere of nostalgia.

"Disha, Kriti… I have to share something with you guys!" said Raghav suddenly, bringing everyone back to the real world, from their thoughts. Riya knew the premise and was prepared for this.

"You are already aware about the current situation with investors. The situation does not look good. I am extremely sorry about this and I could not be guiltier. But VigyaPun is falling apart."

Disha and Kriti had known there were problems. Raghav was seen less in office these days and whenever he did, he was animatedly seen discussing and debating on calls in his cabin. But this sudden announcement left them speechless. They did not know how to react. Raghav could understand what went on in their minds. They deserved to know for having stood by him for all these years.

"This is a heads up. I am sorry, but you guys should start looking for opportunities outside VigyaPun!" Raghav said with a heavy heart as if these were the hardest words he had ever spoken. The gravity of the situation suddenly dawned upon both of them. Riya placed her hand around Disha's shoulder, who sat next to her and looked straight into Kriti's eyes.

These were regular, young millennials with dreams and ambitions in their eyes, who looked up to their company and their founder to lead them. Today, the fear was evident on their faces, as they saw the hopelessness on Raghav's face for the first time in many years. The face that had smiled through the hardest of times, partied as if there was no tomorrow, and was a fire-fighter in everything that happened at VigyaPun. Today, this face had no answers, no motivational words, no hope to give them. It was dead. Blank.

"Is it really that serious?" Disha was the first one to break the silence.

Raghav simply nodded his head and he sadly took another sip of his drink.

"What are you planning then, Raghav?" asked Kriti, still hoping. There was an undying hope that Raghav would come up with a last minute solution as he always did.

Raghav remained silent. The answer was clear, but had to be spoken out. "I don't have any stone left unturned. We have gone out to every possible investor, potential client and tried to figure out every solution possible. But with the mounting costs of the technology end, our investors do not understand that it is sinking us down. Even if we do restructure, it will be as if starting from scratch and we will always have these investors on our back."

Disha and Kriti listened to every word with full attention.

"Raghav…" Disha was the first one to speak after a few minutes of silence. "I speak for myself. Whatever happens, I will stick by you. If this goes down, even though I am sure you will save it like you save everything else, but in case it still goes down, we are all in this together!"

Kriti immediately stepped up. "And so do I. I will be there until the end. I am sure together we will figure out something. I will work on clients and fulfil our promised deliverables, till the very last breath of VigyaPun. I started my career with you Raghav and I will not back off until the end."

Raghav looked at both of them. He had definitely not expected this. The loyalty and faith that they showed in him was moving. He was emotional. He had always believed in keeping people around him happy. In a moment like this, it was the perfect payback.

Riya looked at him and smiled. Raghav smiled back. Putting their careers at stake for VigyaPun, Disha, and Kriti had proved to be the strongest pillars.

Raghav felt indebted to them for having walked the talk on their loyalties towards the company. He had no way to reward them or show them how much it meant.

"That calls for another round of drink, doesn't it?" said Disha, trying to lighten up the mood. As they filled their glasses, Riya gladly exclaimed, "Here is, to brilliant teams that stick together!"

# #15

This was his sixth cup of black coffee in the last hour and half. Raghav impatiently waited in the lobby of the headquarters of Julius Advertisers, one of India's most successful advertising companies that had grown from a startup to a conglomerate in the last eight years. He continuously clicked the lock button of his phone and clicked it again, checking the time like a restless child. He was sweating and the summer heat of North India wasn't helping. The logo of Julius stylishly glowed behind the reception desk. He stared at it for a few minutes.

He was here to explore the last chance to save his company, at the very least give his team and his employees a befitting end and save their livelihoods. Julius Advertisers had reached out to Raghav for a possible acquisition of VigyaPun some months ago, which Raghav had turned down then without even considering. He had never imagined that he would have to go crawling back to the deal.

Raghav was well aware that he had arrived two hours in advance, for the meeting time scheduled with the Executive board and the founding team of Julius. He badly wanted to smoke, but he had promised Riya that he wouldn't, at least not for a month. He tried his best and fought with himself to follow that promise. His phone vibrated softly in his palms and he looked at the notification pop-up. It was a message from Riya – 'I know you must be busy, but I hope everything goes well. This is to say All the Best.'

He closed his eyes for a few seconds. Few sleepless nights, uncountable cups of black coffee, thousands of rows and columns of data in Microsoft Excel, numerous PPTs, comparisons, projections and financials were finally taking a toll and Raghav felt weak from inside. His eyes were puffy and his head felt heavy. He could not help but remember his last visit to Gurgaon just three and half months ago, when he had partied in Cyber Hub. Life had taken a bizarre turn after that, and 'partying' was something other people did – people who did not have start-ups to run and companies to save. The journey of the last three years had been a roller coaster ride, full of passion, enthusiasm, excitement, and celebrations. But life is only a rosy picture till you brush against the thorns.

"Sir…"

Somebody calling out to him, pulled him back to reality. He looked up at the girl sitting at the reception who called him.

"Mr Devraj and the rest of the executive board are ready to meet you. Please proceed towards the board room, the third door to the right."

Raghav took a deep breath, picked up his laptop bag and pulled himself and his thoughts together. While he walked towards the boardroom, another message popped up in the notification centre of his phone. Raghav ignored the message and walked into the boardroom. The room looked like a weird mix of a graveyard and a pub with most of the people either extremely serious or extremely young.

"Let us come straight to the point, Raghav," Devraj, the founder of Julius said in the most straightforward manner Raghav had ever heard. "This acquisition will better be taken as a talent acquisition for us, and we will not be shelling out cash as much, but will be happy to deal in stock options of our company. We need the founder of your company, that is you and we don't really care about the rest."

Raghav did not like the tone of this conversation from the very start. Raghav had been a high-headed, strongly opinionated person, since his teens. He had never liked people bossing him around and had a rebellious streak, which often caused him to react poorly to authoritative displays. He could be polite to people in the nicest of ways, but he could never be subtle in showing his rudeness when people took a bossy tone with him. He fought against his own nature and decided to keep quiet, keeping in mind the sheer gravity of the situation.

"Moreover, we do not deny that you guys have amazing experience and knowledge and that is what is really valuable for this company and our board. We wish to make Julius, a brand of advertising, a platform for advertisers, that is best known even in Tier II and Tier III cities and with your understanding and penetration of this market even with smaller businesses, we could align our aims and work in a common direction."

"Devraj…" said Raghav, clearing his throat and gulping down an entire glass of water before continuing. All eyes in the boardroom remained fixed on him. "Let us make things a little clear here…"

With this very line, Devraj gave him a stern look. Devraj was the supposed poster boy of the Advertising scene of India, which had recently seen a surge in the number of twenty-somethings millionaires.

"I do not want this to be taken as a mere hiring of talent with me coming on board with you. We are selling an idea here, and not ourselves! Moreover, the idea is worth a value and we cannot close down a product overnight that we built up in more than two years, day and night and is still loved by our clients. We were hoping for an 'acquisition' where Julius would of course be willing to continue our brand. Anyways, we are dealing and selling in an untapped market, where we do not compete with core Julius clients. Moreover, our advertising solutions are highly digitized and tech-driven and we believe continuing our brand would not compete with or harm Julius in any way, if it is brought under the same umbrella."

"Raghav… my brother…" said Devraj, almost interrupting him. His non-agreement and contradiction was evident in his sharp eyes and cynical smile. "I do not literally give a rat's ass to the idea and the market. All we need is you, your knowledge, your talent, and your way of dealing in this market. Let us be realistic and talk about acqui-hiring here with no guarantee of a job to each one of your team members unless they prove worthy through an interview and screening process! The brand has to close with no cash exit to the founders!"

Raghav took a deep breath and looked at his empty glass of water. Before he could say anything, Devraj continued, "Your funding news, interviews, and brand features had made it to the front page news of major business magazines and digital news websites some months ago, Raghav! You were almost the most innovative player in the market offering something that none of us could even get into. A startup from Jaipur in Rajasthan, getting this close was a fear that we faced for freaking a year and half," said Devraj and thumped the table with his fist softly.

He looked straight into the eyes of Raghav and continued, "Being in the market, we watch our competitors in the space very closely. I have information that you can never imagine! And trust me; the advertising space is ablaze with the news of the funds' crunch that you are facing. Based on my information from inside sources, I believe you are left with the funds that will last you less than a month. Raghav, I know that you have approached almost every single investor out there for a round of investment, and evidently with no luck! I hope things are clear about who is going to dominate the terms now and who is in need of this deal?"

The entire boardroom fell silent, and the rest of the members provided either their incompetence or their support for Devraj by remaining silent and staring at Devraj in awe. Raghav was blank, and it was not because of the way it was said, but because of what was said. Every word Devraj had said was true. As the peon entered the boardroom and filled the empty glasses of water and served tea and coffee to everyone, Raghav's mind raced with thoughts. Yes, the entire advertising market knew of VigyaPun's funds crunch. The media had already called him a few times for an 'insider' statement, to which he had responded curtly so far.

Raghav looked down at his phone screen, which was placed on the table in front of him and had a sudden rush of adrenaline. He had done over forty meetings in the last two months with no fruitful response so far. He had heard one rejection after another, worded differently but with the same end result. 'We are not looking to invest in this space at the moment'; 'Your traction is not at a range where we could invest, but maybe in a future round we would love to participate' and so many more.

But sometimes, your gut gives you the power to do things that you cannot imagine.

"Devraj…" said Raghav, wearing his black spectacles that he had taken off a few minutes ago. "Two years ago, I started this company with an aim. And let me tell you about that aim, very precisely. We wanted to sell advertising solutions to even the last man standing with extreme ease and a fulfilling experience of reaching their target audience across the world. Today, over five hundred customers love the product that we sell across the country. We sell in cities like Jaipur, Jodhpur, Chandigarh, Kanpur, Lucknow, Guwahati, Pune and in places that you cannot imagine. Tier II and Tier III cities are where India primarily is and I hold over seventy per cent market share in these cities. Even if I have to close down, we will go down with respect and our head held high. If you cannot guarantee hundred per cent job security for my team, this deal is off the table."

The smile on Devraj's face was sarcastic – his eyes remained dead and challenged Raghav to walk out of the boardroom without bowing to his terms.

Raghav picked up his laptop bag and walked out of the boardroom proudly. He was now hardened and ready for the worst.

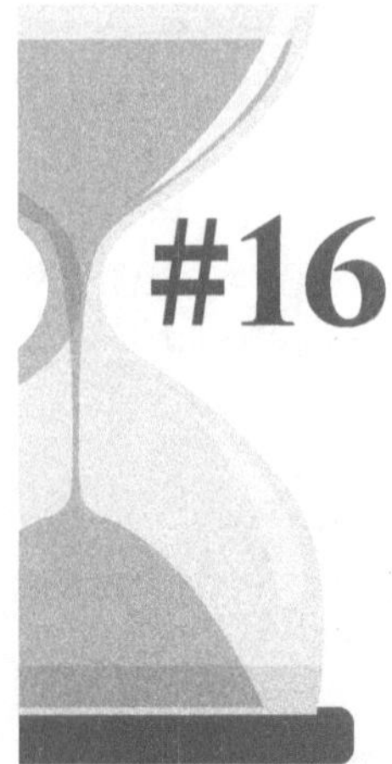

#16

One Month Later

"Raghav, are you okay?" Disha peeped into the cabin and asked innocently. People around Raghav had been talking to him very cautiously in low, soothing tones in the last one month – the kind of tones one uses to visit a sick relative. They were scared of any outburst or mood swing, even though Raghav had been extremely calm and composed throughout. Or at least that is what he had successfully displayed publicly.

There had been nights when he had cried thinking about the last few years. There had been days when he had not left his bed because he did not want to. Just a few months ago, he had never imagined they would be faced with a situation this grim. From a profitable revenue generating startup, VigyaPun had succumbed to changing industry norms, ego-led decisions of investors and some hurried steps of Raghav.

He often contemplated if he could have stepped up and challenged the investors to do things his way. But at the same time, he thought about the pros and cons of having done things his way. In entrepreneurship, there is no right way or wrong way of doing things. A company is built with right people, the right timings, and some decisions that just happen to be proven right.

For a long time, owing to human tendencies, he had tried blaming things on the investors, the city of Delhi, the pressure of deciding to expand to London, even his previous relationship for that matter. He had tried to relieve himself of the guilt by blaming everything around him in moments of loneliness. But there was no running away from the fact that he was as flawed as everything else in the Universe.

Riya had never left his side during the entire period. She did not sugar coat her words, and always pointed out his follies to keep him grounded and face the realities for once. She knew how he would feel about his company, his dream crashing down.

He was a first generation entrepreneur and the risks that come with the tag were unimaginable. A lot was at stake and he had nothing to fall back on. The biggest human challenge was of course, keeping his mind stable, his mental health in check and still facing his team every day in office.

He saw Disha peeping in from the cabin door.

"Of course, pop in!" said Raghav, sounding cheerful, as he

closed a few folders laid out on his table.

"Raghav, you have already referred almost everyone in the team to some other company. What really is the plan?" asked Disha, sounding scared.

Raghav smirked. "Do I have an option, Disha? You have always known everything."

"This was your dream, Raghav. This was your blood and sweat. You have let it slip away so easily."

"Easily? You think?"

"You know what I meant!"

"Disha, I have given everything to this company. I left my city, my family, my girlfriend, my friends, everyone behind. In the last four months, I have tried everything I could."

"Fuck this recession and the sudden downfall in the startup ecosystem."

"Can't blame it on anything, Disha. It was a mix of bad decisions, wrong timing and of course, unpreparedness."

"But even giants have fallen. Huge companies have reported bankruptcy. You know that…"

"Yes, but a lot of them have survived this period as well, and are going to. Unfortunately, we won't be one of them. And I feel sorry for every team member…"

"You have referred everyone already and personally ensured that each one of them has a job."

"That is the least I could do. All the relationships and network that I have built in all these years had to pay off somewhere. At least, they did here!" Raghav smiled. Disha looked at him sadly.

She remembered all those times when they had sat alone in a small 200 sq. ft. office in Jaipur, their hometown. Flashbacks in her mind replayed all those moments when Raghav used to crack a client and they used to celebrate. How they hired their first employee—from then on, in no time, life moved at a rocket pace—from Jaipur to Delhi, from a small office to a plush corporate building. All the challenges and how they overcame it together as a team, flashed in Disha's mind and she looked at Raghav blankly. Their rapid growth into the Tier II and III towns of India and about how their clients would send in amazing feedback of their experience had all been like a dream come true.

The biggest achievement in creating a new company is to create something that people love. VigyaPun had done that effectively.

"I need to wrap up the legal work as well in the next one week, otherwise, it will become a pain in the ass," said Raghav, sorting his folders back in the rack.

"Can I help with something… anything?" asked Disha, desperate to support Raghav. She had seen him toil day and night for this company, since the very first day. She had known him too well, to let him go through this alone. She thought about the broader aspect –hundreds of companies face such situations and close. What goes through those hundreds of entrepreneurs who built these companies? The mental trauma that they go through—this was no less than the loss of a close one.

"Uh! Actually, there is...."

"Yes, tell me please!"

"You know we renewed the rent deed of this office a few months ago. We have a lock-in of two more months. You are on good terms with Mr Kelkar. If you can talk to him and request him for a waiver... because bearing the rent of this office for two more months without any inflow would be a huge setback."

"I completely forgot that we would be letting go of this office as well..." said Disha, shocked within herself, as if it was a part of her life that had to be given away. She remembered the party they had thrown when they had shifted to this office two years ago. The who's who of the startup ecosystem, media, family, and friends had been invited and it was a grand launch. No one, in their darkest dreams, could have imagined then that this day would come.

"Uh, yes! This office was a happy place. It has seen its heyday and been a part of this company as much as you and me. But it has to go as well..."

"Hmm... sure, I will have a chat with Mr Kelkar tomorrow, first thing in the morning. Don't worry about it. I will call it a day for today... I want to go back to my apartment and just be alone for some time..."

Disha packed her bag to leave. Raghav gave her a meek smile.

"Disha, what is your plan?" asked Raghav, something that he had been thinking about a lot. "I have told you, I can refer you somewhere really good. You have a great experience. You are no less than a co-founder of this company, in any way. Any company would value you…"

"Thanks a lot, Raghav. I will of course let you know, whenever I need that referral. For now, I want to take a break, go back to Jaipur, and just let it all sink in."

Raghav nodded. He could understand how Disha felt. She was the first employee of the company and she witnessed the downfall of the company she had built as well. The helplessness showed on her face. The desperation of being of any help possible was evident and it was humbling for Raghav. She had often mentioned in lighter moments that this would be the company and the work, which she would stick to until her life ends. Raghav wished he could create a company like that.

The depth of the void in his mind was deepening day by day. He dreaded the moment when he would have to finally pack up and call it the end. The only thing keeping his sanity right now was his relationship with Riya. The strength that he got from her was unmatchable. The emptiness was sometimes on the verge of horror, when he could literally hear the silence inside and around him. Many times during this period at his house, which had been the hub of parties and happiness, he could sense the silence creeping in around him. At late hours of the night, he preferred increasing the volume of his speakers to maximum, as if music would fill the void and replace his mood. Whatever helps! He often thought to himself.

His utmost priority was making sure that everyone was placed somewhere and had been taken care of. With whatever team he had, he wanted to also take care of the client deliverables. Clients who had stuck until the end and maintained relations were of extreme value to Raghav. He ensured they were also provided a suitable backup to ensure that their operations were not impacted. These things kept him awake. Things went around in circles in his mind.

And then the scaring thought of being back home, of facing his own family, who had always trusted him and had undying faith in him that he would take the right decision and was mature enough to do his own thing. He remembered his parents who were shocked with his decision to resign from a well-settled, high paying consulting job. It killed him inside throughout many nights, just the thought of facing them again.

He had stopped meeting his old friends in the last couple of months. Just as Keshav had marked him as the 'Startup Poster Boy' from their entire batch, many of his friends had always looked up to his decision of following the passion. He would be a laughing stock for them. No one understood failures. No one celebrates downfalls. All that people see are the multi-million funding stories in the Media and the glittery Startup Events.

Raghav and his deep gulf of guilt and self-deprecation had taken him into another world, which happened almost the entire day now. Disha's sudden question brought him back with a jolt.

"If I may ask you, what is your plan?" asked Disha, after a few seconds of pause as if reading his mind.

Raghav smiled again, looking at her.

"Honestly, I have not given it a thought. I want to pack up everything, sit back, and watch it go like the Titanic..."

"Why don't you come back to Jaipur? Stay at home, free your mind a bit..." Disha suggested, genuinely concerned for him.

"I did tell my parents about everything, last night. I give them all the updates anyway. They were quite worried themselves. Their worries would only increase if I go back to Jaipur and sit at home with no plans for the near future."

"It is better than being alone here, Raghav."

"Thanks a lot for the concern, Disha. Amidst all the negativity and darkness here in Delhi, there might actually be a fair reason for me to stay for some time..." said Raghav and winked as his phone beeped with a message from Riya Bansal – *We are on for tonight, right? 8.30 pm at Social?*

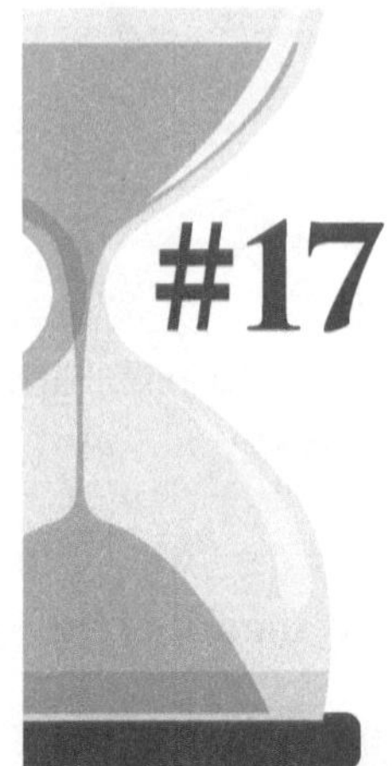

#17

Away from the world, in each other,
They found solace
Moments slowed down, the time moved leisurely,
Shutting out the world's race

Unfortunately, Raghav and Riya's relationship had a bumpy start, considering the phase that Raghav was going through professionally. Many nights went by just talking to Riya about the entire fiasco he was facing. And she heard all of it patiently. He knew he was not at the best of his demeanour and behaviour, but Riya took everything surprisingly pleasantly.

They talked about a million things in the world, and she was the only reason that Raghav used to laugh during this period. He never said it aloud, but if Riya had not come into his life at the right time, the repercussions might have been worse. It is a mark of strong-willed humans—they always find their solace in something at the time of disaster, to avoid falling down. For Raghav, that solace was Riya—an excuse to continue fighting, to live.

They had started meeting regularly five or six months ago.

Their meetings were the happiest space for Raghav—the only space where he could truly be himself. He did not have to put on a garb of being strong; he did not have to disguise himself as a superhuman entrepreneur, who would take care of everything. The best company to be in is the one where you don't always have to be the winner. If you cannot show your fears, failures and weaknesses in front of someone, they are truly not the best company you ever had.

Their meetings were a lot more than mere hangouts, and a little less than what could be defined as a date. Both were happy to keep it that way. Besides, the entire situation Raghav was in, there was a mutual unsaid understanding, of not hurrying too much into something. Best relationships do not start at the time of vulnerability.

"Coincidentally, I got an invite to attend a seminar in Jaipur as a Speaker today."

"Really? When is it?"

"In two weeks… And I thought, since you do not have a lot on your hands these days, you could be a great company for me in your own city!"

"That is a very dark remark to make to someone who has a company falling down!" Raghav said with a smile and took a sip from his drink. The dim-lit ambience overlooking the Hauz Khas Lake and the soulful Sufi music playing at the terrace of Social, made a perfect setup for a conversation.

"I am kidding..." Riya said laughing. "But tell me, will you accompany me? I am speaking on the Innovating and

Revolutionising traditional businesses for the future…"

"A perfect topic for all those with a silver spoon. Jaipur will have your target market!"

"So you are saying I was born with a silver spoon! I actually am trying to revolutionize my family's business of clothing."

"I am not saying that… Just saying that you have it easier than most people trying to start something of their own!"

"Just because we got a head start does not mean we don't face business challenges. You guys in the 'startup' ecosystem seem to think as if all the wrath of the three worlds has fallen upon you!"

Raghav laughed. "The eternal debate of nepotism—I will not get into that. I was just trying to work you up. I completely agree with what you are saying anyway…but you look cute when you are all worked up!"

Riya blushed and tried to avoid Raghav's eyes by taking a few long sips of her drink.

"So, during all this mess, did you get time to write something?" Riya asked all of a sudden.

"Not a bit. You think I am in the headspace of writing romantic poetry right now!"

"Romantic poetry does not need headspace. It needs a reason," said Riya and winked at him.

"Ahan!" Raghav exclaimed. "I shall try my hand at it soon then, now that you have motivated me. It has actually been ages since I wrote something!"

Raghav realised as he said it. It had been months since he had given any time to his creative space. Having come out of a toxic relationship, thinking about business day and night and then facing tough times, all of this had mentally drained him. He thought about those nights' years ago, when he used to wake up and write poems. He missed writing. He missed how he had written a poem for a friend's cafe that had gone viral on social media. He missed his 'own' time. He wanted it back. He wanted to be in his zone. He wanted to think ahead. While sitting with Riya in the soothing ambience of Social, he realised he wanted to come out of VigyaPun's failure and look ahead in life. But, look at what? For more than three years of his life, he had only thought about one thing. How could it be so easy for him to simply accept that it was over?

"So, did you?" Riya's sudden change of topic pulled him out of this loop. Raghav had been going into these loops very often these days.

"Did I what?" Raghav asked, startled.

"Disha's question... Did you decide on what you will do now?" Riya asked, looking at him with deep intensity in her eyes.

Raghav pulled his thoughts together, and without any second thought, replied, "Varanasi... I will go to Varanasi for a few days to take a break..."

#18

Sometimes, instinct works in weird ways and takes you places. Two days after that meeting with Riya at Social, Raghav found himself on the flight to Varanasi. Visiting Varanasi had been on Raghav's mind for a long time. The rush and pace of his life had not allowed him to take a break. He had no memory of a lone quality break that he had taken in recent years. He read a thriller on his flight picked up from the airport shop, another thing that he had not done since long.

He occasionally peeped out of the window to admire the beauty of the clouds and the view. No matter how high you rise, you should always have time to stop and appreciate the beauty of the world around you. Life is truly no fun without enjoying the things that you earn with hard work.

Raghav checked into the backpackers' hostel. He had firmly decided to keep the trip as raw and earthy as possible. No hotels, no cabs and a lot of alone time – he had promised himself. It was evening by the time he settled down in the hostel's dorm. He went to the common room to check out the place.

He found a chair in the balcony of the hostel that was truly made for young travellers. A well-designed common room, with beanbags and a cute balcony, bunk beds in the dormitories, and a prime located property, it was a great place to immerse yourself in some serious thinking about life. He smoked with his evening tea in solace, as he watched the sun drown in River Ganga in the far distance.

A group of four youngsters entered the common room, having a hearty laugh about something. There was something familiar about the girl in the group. Seemingly in her early thirties, smartly dressed in casuals, she looked confident and sharp. Raghav's brain could not connect, but he definitely found something familiar about her.

As if a tradition, they immediately came to him and greeted him with handshakes introducing themselves. Before the three men finished introducing themselves and the girl put her hand forward, Raghav suddenly connected the strings and immediately said, "Dakshi? Dakshi Dave…"

"Uh! I am flattered…" she replied humbly.

"Founder of *WomenUp!* What a coincidence!" Raghav exclaimed.

Dakshi was one of the most popular faces of the startup ecosystem of India. Her company ran a community platform for empowering women, by helping them sell their products, offer support in terms of health, career, violence, abuse etc. WomenUp was one of the first unicorns to have come out of the country backed up by some of the biggest investor networks of the world. Dakshi was a startup star. Raghav could not believe his fate. He had heard her talks, attended her seminars, watched her interviews, and followed her on social networks.

"Pleasure meeting you… uh…" Dakshi said, indicating that he had completely forgotten to introduce himself.

"Raghav. I am the Founder of an AdTech…" he stopped in the middle of his sentence. This was the first time he had to formally introduce himself to someone after the closure of his company. He had never faced a situation so awkward. Suddenly, he realised he had no identity. VigyaPun was his identity. He was nothing without his company. He went into a sudden tunnel of darkness, demotivation and under-confidence. His stomach churned.

"Excuse me… I am getting a call…" Raghav stammered and rushed to his dorm room.

He straightaway went to the washroom and looked in the mirror. Who was he? What was his identity? How would he introduce himself? How would people perceive his failure? Would they judge him? Was this a question mark on his leadership and skills?

He sat in the washroom for what seemed to be like an eternity. Thankfully, he did not puke as he had expected. He felt like a grown up. He felt as if he had aged suddenly after everything he had seen in the past few months. He washed his face and mustered the courage to walk out again. It was already late evening by then and he hoped that the common room would be empty.

He walked across the common room and spotted Dakshi sitting alone working on her laptop in a corner. He walked past her as if he didn't notice her and hoped that she would not notice him either. He went to the balcony and lit up a smoke.

"Can I have the lighter as well?" said Dakshi from behind, as she came into the balcony.

"Oh! Dakshi, hey! Of course…" he said, trying to sound pleasantly surprised.

"So, you were telling us about your startup…" she said, sounding genuinely interested. The thing about being a part of the ecosystem is that everyone wants to know and probe into your story.

Raghav was silent for a few seconds. As she smoked, Dakshi looked extremely calm and wise. Some people carry optimism with them in their demeanour. She was one of them.

Without any second thoughts, Raghav pulled himself together and said, "Yeah… VigyaPun. It was an AdTech company that I had founded three years ago. Actually, we could not sustain any further and closed down last month…" He said, almost as if preparing himself with an introduction that he would have to use a lot in the coming days.

"Uh! So how was the learning?" Dakshi asked within a second, as if she was prepared with the question. The question was intriguing – not something you would expect immediately when you tell them about your failed startup – even before condolences for your fallen business. Raghav was taken aback, but he smiled. So did Dakshi.

"That…" said Raghav, still unsure how to answer that. It was one question that made him look back at his entire tenure of three years, on what he had gained and so much that he had sacrificed and lost. He questioned whether it was worth it. Dakshi's question was positively interesting. Raghav suddenly realised that it was after all, not bad. The experiences he had, the people he met, the conferences where he spoke to a crowd of thousands, the media stories – it was all probably worth it. The entire learning from creating something from scratch with no backing from your family or friends was inexplicable. The happiness of cracking that first client of your new company matches no celebration. The contentment of having built something on your own, creating a team that you can swear by, a client base that truly respects and loves your product – it was satisfying in a weird way.

Amidst all the misery and sorrow of shutting down his baby and facing people after the failure, this was the first time Raghav looked at the bright side of the entire experience. He knew the journey from here was going to be even more challenging and tough. Corporates don't look at ex-startup founders as worthy for jobs because they are always at a flight risk owing to their entrepreneurial streak. Nor is it easy to start up again in an ecosystem, which is ruthless, and owned by vultures. India was far behind in the maturity of the startup ecosystem. In India, people invested on faces and degrees, and not on ideas.

Every startup ecosystem has its own lifecycle, where it goes through the entire process of attaining maturity. India was at a cusp, making things even more difficult for new entrants.

Despite the challenges that awaited him, Raghav felt uplifted suddenly with the experiences he had gained and the relationships that he was carrying with him. Putting all his thoughts together, he finally tried to articulate it to Dakshi.

"Uh…that was good but painfully so… I learned…a lot about everything and not just business."

"Yeah!" Dakshi exclaimed, almost with uncanny excitement. "Learned about life, eh?"

"Surprisingly, yes. But you know, at the end of it, I am a failure…" Raghav said sadly.

"How old are you, Raghav?"

"I am 28…"

"Brilliant! I am 36, and you know about the success of WomenUp," Dakshi said confidently. "You admire my work, you follow me on social media, and you think I am popular. But do you know what I did before WomenUp?"

"Uh… No," said Raghav, trying to remember anything about her previous experiences from any interview.

"That is the best thing about life, Raghav. People tend to forget your failures and past, but they always appreciate you for your present. No one is going to remember this phase after a few weeks…and trust me, not even you. Your past is not going to affect your future from here on…unless you let it," said Dakshi. She patted him on his back and went away to her room leaving Raghav with a cloud of smoke, a million thoughts and a good feeling.

Raghav sat there in the balcony for what seemed like ages. He watched the dim lights of the Ghats of Varanasi visible in the near distance. He took deep breaths almost as if trying to inhale the vibe of the city. He thought about what Dakshi said. There had been times when he wanted to end everything and just run away and then there was Riya, who motivated him to keep going and think about the people around him.

Dakshi was right. Raghav thought about people who inspired him. He did not know their back stories and their failures. Raghav had to think ahead. With his current mind set, it seemed impossible. But he had to start moving forward. He was only 28! He repeated to himself.

He had to fight the circumstances and come out as a survivor. He could not succumb to this one experience. His dreams and his experiences were bigger than this. But starting up again and going through the entire pain of setting up a business seemed to be like cliff-climbing right now. He had no clue about his next step and that made him uncomfortable.

He decided to give some rest to his mind. He took a few deep breaths again, stretched out his legs, and fell asleep in the balcony itself.

#19

The forsaken future,
The forbidden fate
Destiny playing
The devil's advocate

The streets of Varanasi remind you of a game of Pacman, with lanes that have no destination, with random twists and turns and scenes that you might not be able to witness anywhere across the world. In the early hours of the day, the peculiar smell of the narrow streets mixed with the aroma of fresh food being fried was an amazing thing to experience.

Having stopped for a glass of *lassi,* Raghav was surprised and intrigued by the number of dead bodies that passed by and how normal it was for the people of the city.

"Varanasi is truly the city of death as much as it is for life," he quipped to the snack shop owner.

"Death, here, is a celebration Sir…" the shop owner replied matter of factly. "And why should it not be? What is all this for, after all?"

"Uh?" Raghav was confused. Either all of this was too simple or way too complex at once.

"Yes sir! You and me, our lives, our successes and failures, our ups and downs… does it really matter? It all comes down to this at the end," the shop owner had a huge grin on his face as he pointed behind Raghav. He turned around and saw another dead body being carried away by a few people.

"This is the most peaceful that a man can ever be. It is a celebration indeed, Sir," the shop owner continued his pearls of wisdom, despite no response from Raghav.

Raghav with the fear of coming across as rude and uninterested decided to probe further. "So, you think it is good that your city is regarded as a perfect place to 'die', instead of anything else?"

The shop owner gave a hearty laugh, without taking any offense. "When Lord Shiva himself had severed off one of Brahma's heads during a fight, he carried it in his hand as an act of ignominy. Only when he arrived in Varanasi, the head dropped off from his hand and vanished beneath the ground. That is how holy this land is for the dead, Sir…"

"And you believe this to be true?"

"No no, sir! I am too small a mortal to believe or disbelieve anything. Belief is for mythology, for religion, for God. But Shiva is one of us. He is in you and me. He is everywhere. But, have you visited Dashashwamedh yet?"

"Uh yes, got a chance to attend the *Aarti* yesterday! It was truly mesmerizing," said Raghav. The shop owner smiled gleefully as if Raghav had appreciated one of his own creations.

The experience of understanding the belief that a city local could have in his city's rich heritage and culture was refreshing. The mere excitement of his conversation was infectious. Raghav stepped back from his shop to take leave. He realised he had a happy smile on his face. Was it the morning or a quick chat with a loyal city local? Or was it the city itself? It was relieving. Maybe it was about being away from all the chaos that he had left behind.

As he checked his phone in his pocket to find his way out of the street, the shop owner called out behind him. "Sir, this lane ends straight at the Manikarnika Ghat. That is where Shiva lost his earring while taking a swim. Manikarnika witnesses more than 300 cremations a day, Sir. It is worth a visit!"

Raghav shook his head with a smile as he waved back at him. The irony of the last sentence of the shop owner itself was the uniqueness of this weirdly and uncannily peaceful city of Varanasi. The strong belief of every person, about how Shiva was a part of their everyday lives, their being and their surroundings was just unbelievable. Was he, really? Here, he was worried about the failure of his company and the grim future that awaited him. And this was an entire city celebrating something as dark as death like a carnival. Such was the irony of the world.

Nonetheless, a few hours later, as the sun set beautifully into the soothing River Ganga, he found himself sitting in a corner at the Manikarnika Ghat. In the last couple of minutes, he had seen numerous bodies being burnt to ashes as per the Hindu rituals. He tried keeping a mental count, but lost track in between as his mind wandered from one thought to another.

He felt awkwardly peaceful and relaxed. He felt guilty at the same time to be finding relaxation amidst bodies being cremated. He took out his phone and called Riya. They had been in constant touch since the last few days. To think of it, there were only two things that Raghav really missed away from the mayhem of the world – walking into his own office every morning and Riya Bansal. The strange part was that one had abandoned him completely and the other had held on to him despite his failures.

"Riya, I never imagined it would be like this…these last few days here," he told her about his sumptuous lassi and spicy conversation with the shop owner and his time at Manikarnika.

"And you are sure, you don't want your 'me' time right now?" Riya asked him. The best part about her was that she knew exactly when Raghav wanted to be left alone.

"I find my 'me' time in my time with you as well…" Raghav replied.

"But this is really interesting. So finally in the city of death, you feel alive," said Riya with a smirk.

"Truly…like never before! As I sit here, I can feel every breath and every second passing by as if I own it."

"And I am glad to hear this unearthly charm and calm in your voice after so long!"

"I am glad to hear your voice, while I look at this scenery in front of my eyes," said Raghav. They shared a few moments of long distance romance.

"So did you finally get time and mental space to think about, what next?" Riya asked him, with a mix of concern and intrigue.

"Actually, no! To be honest, I decided not to think about it for now even if I have the time. I feel my mind is relaxed and lifted off from these things after a long time. I feel as if the breeze is filling up the void inside me. And I want to feel this. Somehow, I don't want to spend this time thinking about the sorrows of my past and the suspense of my future."

"Hmm! Makes sense, but as you promised, do find time to write something on this trip," said Riya, once again reminding him and pushing him to get back to the one thing he truly loved.

They had a soft and calm conversation, as the water of Ganga turned darker with the dusk. Few boats still rowed after the evening Aarti and Manikarnika Ghat got less busy as minutes passed by. Only some *pandits* and shopkeepers went around doing their daily chores at the end of the day, only to start a night full of life.

"Riya..." Raghav called out softly as their conversation came to a close. "I love you..."

There was silence for a few seconds— silence that pierced through every nerve of Raghav's body.

"Is it the vibe of your current surrounding or..."

"It is you, and only that," Raghav replied instantly, without waiting for her to finish her question.

Riya took a deep breath. "I love you too, Raghav and I can't wait to see you soon…"

They hung up with the confession of love for the first time. Confessing your feelings to someone is the weirdest part. You feel good about having let out your feelings and also having them reciprocated. But at the same time you feel jittery about what awaits you now. The excitement and butterflies of a new relationship, doing everything for the first time with someone, the giddiness of old school romance can never get clichéd.

For Raghav, it was an interesting space—ending something so close to him—and starting something with someone so close. These two extreme emotions clashed inside him, as did the small waves of the river with the ghats. The excitement and agog inside him on being in a relationship with Riya was no less a feeling than starting a new venture. The kick he got from entrepreneurship—the curiosity, the dedication, the undying feeling of passion—was so similar to what he felt right now about the relationship. And at the same time, he fought the battle against falling into the deep abyss that VigyaPun had brought upon him.

These were extreme ends of the same spectrum. He had met Riya during a literal debacle in his life when he was on tenterhooks about the bare survival of his company. Yet Riya had stuck with him, faced all his mood swings and aberrant behaviour. He had repeatedly, tried to give her the best, but was unfortunately faced by the continuous upheaval of his venture – his baby that he had nurtured with his blood, sweat, and savings.

Riya's understanding about his emotions and his comfort in her presence attracted Raghav more. He could not be without her. A simple phone call for a few minutes could keep him going for a day. Her words meant the world to him.

With her motivation, he now wanted to go back to his hometown. He had felt embarrassed to face his parents, to have squashed their dreams for him and disappointed their belief. But Riya made him see that one thing he needed right now was to be in his comfort zone. Jaipur, his home, his family were definitely his most comfortable space.

As Raghav thought about all of this amidst the uncertainty of his professional life, he heard behind him, "Ganga doesn't give you answers unless you are Bhishma Pitamah!"

Raghav turned around and laughed at the remark of Dakshi. She stood right behind him with a smoke, as she stared at the farthest end as well.

"It sure doesn't. But it does let you drown your sorrows pretty well!"

"Does it?" She quipped. "I will try sometime…"

She sat down next to him and handed him the cigarette for a puff. He took one and gave it back.

"So, what have you thought next?"

"Uh! You almost read my mind!" said Raghav, sounding surprised.

"Oh, it is not a gift or anything. Just experiences and stories put together with a bit of good human observation."

"I have no clue. I have looked up a few job openings on LinkedIn, though. But everything just seems so run-of-the mill."

"Ahan! Job openings, tell me about it…"

"You know what I mean! Sometimes, I feel I am the best fit for a business profile, with my sales skills. But then, I am a Chartered Accountant and finance would any day be my calling…"

"But in your own company, you were getting to do all of it… fulfil all your roles. Be what you want on whatever day!"

"Exactly! But that is not an option now, right?" Raghav said sadly, looking at Dakshi.

"Who says? You ran a business successfully for three years. Entrepreneurship is your calling…"

"Successfully?"

"Yes, you 'ran' it. You put together a team, which I am sure, loved working for you. You cracked business; you created a name for yourself."

"Yes, but I cannot afford to start something again and lose all of it yet again! I can't go through this ever again in my life."

"Wow! You are so certain that you will fail again. I am not asking you to start anything just for the sake of it. Wait for the opportunity," Dakshi said animatedly.

"And do what? Sit and just wait for it?"

"No! Prepare for it. Read stuff, pursue your hobbies, do what you never did due to lack of time, attend events, conferences, meet people…Phew! You can do so much in this time. And you never know where the opportunity will come from or when that apple will fall on your head!"

"And you know what troubles me day and night?"

"What is it, Raghav?"

"How do I know? What if I am not a good entrepreneur in the first place?"

"Hmm! Interesting…" Dakshi smiled, and ready with her pearls of wisdom continued, "There is no litmus test. The only thing I see that I can share with you is that you have the hunger. You wake up hungry and you sleep hungry. And this hunger is for passion, for dreams that are bigger than any of us can imagine."

"And what if those dreams are way out of my reach?"

"Raghav, daring to dream is the first step towards fulfilling the dream. You left your consulting career – that is daring! People talk about dreams, they write about them, they post motivational quotes on social media and yet, they do not take such a step as you did!"

Raghav thought about it. And Dakshi continued, "And you know what! You love your own space. And a true entrepreneur needs to do things alone, on his own, day in and day out! You love your isolation from the rest of the noise and that makes you different. This – right here – this isolation is where you will find all the answers!"

Raghav nodded, agreeing to a certain extent as Dakshi's words seeped in his mind, making sense one by one.

"Raghav, go ahead, spend some time on your own as you are doing right now and the answers will come to you. Entrepreneurship or job, there is no bias. But don't take your decisions when you are reeling from a loss. Wait for the right time and then decide!"

Raghav remained silent for a while. He was calculating mentally. He knew he had enough savings to spend some time on his own. But could he risk starting a business again? Going through the entire process of setting up a new business, with the doubled fear of failure, just felt too much. He was not ready at all. The last two months had instilled doubt and fear in him – changed him into a fearful person.

His mind almost overflowed with his thoughts and he spoke, whispering his biggest fear. "But what about everyone? People talk, they observe, they watch…what will they think of me? That I am unemployed?"

Dakshi got up, rubbed the dust off her hands, and turned around to leave as she said, "Dude, now that you know they are watching, at least put up a good show for them!"

#20

Heavy unexpected rains welcomed Raghav and Riya in Jaipur. As their early morning train pulled into the railway station, they rushed to their cab covering their heads with their hands enjoying every moment, as they laughed enraptured by the rain. Raghav had imagined that a train journey could be this fun, with casual playful conversations and the watery tea of the Indian Railways.

Their cab sped towards Jaipur Marriott where Riya was staying to drop her off. As the cab went past JLN Road, the prime road connecting all the major areas of Jaipur, Raghav surrendered to the feelings of nostalgia. The city meant so much to him. The sudden feeling of being 'home' engulfed him. The city was where he had lived the majority of his life so far, grown up, made friends, and built a career. This was home to his family. Every corner, every building had a memory of its own.

The staggering World Trade Park stood stylishly visible from a distance looking majestic. Clouds had engulfed the morning sky and it was dark as if the evening was already settling in. Rains lashed against the windshield as numerous walkers and two-wheelers took shade under bus stands and huge trees on the pathways.

The traffic, which was anyways less compared to larger cities, was even thinner because of the rains. The usual office crowd had evidently not left their homes due to the rains. The smell of damp sand filled their senses, wafting in from the slightly open cab windows. The pleasant weather seemed to make everyone happy as the cab driver played some romantic songs. People standing stranded in the pathways had no regret on their faces as they also enjoyed the rains washing away their plans for the day. That was the spirit of this city. Rains meant everything good.

Raghav remembered those long chats and calls when friends would call up and make plans to go to a fort or some rooftop cafe as soon as the clouds gathered. Those bike rides across the city, a cup of tea at the roadside *thadi*, and the comfort of a place where everyone would know you.

In no time, the cab pulled into the driveway of Marriott. "So, I see you in two hours?" Raghav asked.

"Go home; spend time with your family. I have a presentation to complete, if you don't remember! I have to speak tomorrow."

"Of course! Let's meet post-lunch and I will show you around?"

"Done deal!"

"And you are coming home tomorrow after the talk!" said Raghav, as he changed the destination in the App to his home.

Raghav entered his home, almost after six months. Last time he had been to his home after his London trip, it had been all rosy. Life was good and he had a happy weekend spending time with his parents. His Jaipur office had also been functional. The office was a modest one-room space and had five employees, working on technology backend and customer support centre. He had let them go last month and helped them be placed in a software development company of his old friend from the ecosystem in Jaipur itself.

He remembered that he had to visit the office to clear up the pending things. He noted it down in his Reminders List, which now mostly consisted of things related to the legalities of shutting down the company.

Having started his business from this city, Jaipur was special to him. The closely-knit and small startup ecosystem recognised him as one of the poster boys of entrepreneurship in the city. His popular hangout spots, tea joints, office buildings, everywhere he knew people and they knew about his work and the success story of VigyaPun. This gave him jitters and the mere thought of facing the same people again had kept him away from his hometown during the last month.

He spent two good hours with his parents in their bedroom talking about everything that had happened. He told them of the investor pressures, letting go of the smaller clients and about how the investors did not let the technology aspect go away that ultimately led to the company's downfall. Whether it was his wrong decisions in the early stage of the company or the ego clashes of the investors that resulted in this fiasco was debatable. But he skipped that part and finally told them about the decision of shutting down.

Fortunately, Raghav had a progressive and understanding family. They had been supportive of his entrepreneurial dreams since the first day having told him upfront that business is not in the family, so they would not be able to extend any help. His father, being the disciplinarian that he was, had told him that he should stand on his own feet now and not expect anything from them, except their mental support for him. He still remembered the clear day when in the same room and the same setup he had told them, that he is leaving his job to pursue his entrepreneurial dreams.

His sister, who now lived in Melbourne with her husband, had been another strong pillar of his life. Her undying love for him was his unsaid support at all times. She remained on Facetime Call throughout his discussion at home and listened intently, as she knew the entire story already.

Raghav often called her from his home's balcony ranting about a week or fortnight's happenings to her. Few months ago, she had told him on one such call, *we are always there to have your back. You are the youngest in the family and you should have all the right to experiment, make mistakes, fall, and then rise again.*

He had cried after the call thinking about how he had been blessed with people around him. Such incidents often reiterated his thinking of how it is the people around you, who impact your life the maximum and truly make or break a person.

After his ordeal, his sister was the first to speak as expected.

"Raghav, it is fine. These are mere experiences that are a part of life. And you are just 28, for God's sake. And you know what; you have the opportunity and chance to make mistakes."

Her words uplifted him as they always had since childhood. He felt as if a huge weight was being lifted off his shoulders. The weirdest part in life is that no matter how supportive your family is, you always live with a constant fear of letting them down. No matter where in the world and what you do, there is a constant feeling of making them proud and proving yourself to them. Probably that is how Indian upbringing is. The competitive landscape of education, the cutthroat competition you grow in and the pressures that a family faces while raising a kid imbibes a sense of insecurity in your mind by default. Thus, her words meant a lot more than what they were.

His fear of putting his parents through shame, the insecurity of letting the confidence of his sister in him break down suddenly washed away and he felt relieved, as he never had in the past few weeks. During his trip to Varanasi, he had realised from the words of Dakshi that probably, he would never be able to work for someone else ever again. He was not built for that. And today, the words of his family relieved him off the penance that he had been inflicting on himself through this time.

"Businesses take time to build, my son. They rise and fail. You are giving yourself too much importance if you think it was all because of you. Hundreds of external factors affect the running of a business. Things did not work in your favour this time and that is completely fine!" his father said with a smile. Putting it in the simplest of words, he made the deepest impact in Raghav's mind.

The conversation lasted long before the real question came up.

"So what are you planning to do now? Should I ask Yatin to look for an opportunity for you?" his mother asked, referring to one of her college friends, who now headed an FMCG multinational in Mumbai. Everyone went silent, waiting for his answer.

"Uh actually... I did get a lot of time to think about it in Varanasi." Raghav hesitated a bit while answering. "I want to take some time and think about a business opportunity, if possible."

Few seconds of silence seeped in and his father looked at him. Out of a sudden hesitation, Raghav said, "And... and I have enough savings to start something. You guys don't have to worry even a bit," he said reassuringly.

He looked at everyone in turn before his father got up from the bed and said, "Raghav, I have always said this and I will just reiterate. You are a brilliant boy. I do not have a single ounce of doubt about your capability of running a business. You have time on your side. Go ahead. We always have your back..." He said walking to him, ruffled his hair with love and left the room to continue with his daily chores. Raghav was left with a sense of gratitude and respect for the kind of family he had grown up in.

He often met young entrepreneurs, who did not receive the

same kind of support from their families and often let their dreams die because of the lack of mental support. This was a problem deeper than it seemed. This created an entire chain of mindset, where thousands of youngsters every year were thrown into the regular jobs that the society expected them to do. With dreams, many innovative ideas also die. Raghav thought about the entire ripple effect and then imagined how his life would have been, had he not received this support from his family.

He finally decided to move ahead and start thinking about his next move. The question loomed over him like a sword.

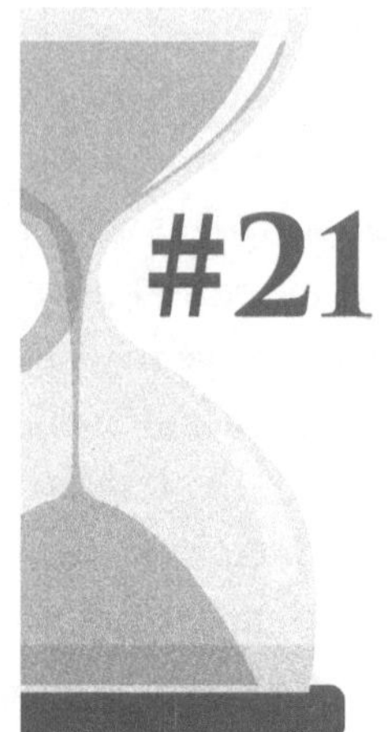

#21

Riya's talk went off really well. Listeners loved her insights on traditional businesses going modern, and she networked with numerous new people. This was a completely new geography for her and she was excited to be a part of this event. And even more so, excited to be in Jaipur with Raghav.

As Raghav enjoyed a cup of tea in the networking area of the event, she was surrounded by a couple of middle-aged women, who were seemingly impressed with her experience and achievements at that age. Raghav smiled and enjoyed from a distance. He was used to this kind of attention. The kick and the vibe of coming down from a stage after a terrific talk to be surrounded by a crowd of people, wanting to talk to you or exchange business cards. In fact, co-incidentally, Riya and he had first met at such an event itself in New Delhi.

The sheer thrill of being the core attention of a room was what he really missed. Hundreds of startup and business events happened every week across the country, and yet in the last three months he had not been to even a single one. He terribly missed that stage and longed to hold that mike again. He had no idea when he would get to do that again. Or will he, ever? He did not even know what he was going to do next. While he had everyone close to him in confidence about his entrepreneurial aspirations, he still considered taking up a job, moving to another country, starting fresh in whatever way he could.

But today, he was content. He felt happy seeing this happen with Riya. He was elated to see her being the centre of attention as he sipped his cup of tea. The only person he could share everything with, all his bare feelings and thoughts was Riya.

She walked towards him, dressed smartly in a business suit carrying her wallet.

"So? How did it go?" she asked nervously.

"Seriously? This modesty, eh! That crowd already is a testimony to how it went!" Raghav exclaimed, pointing to the group of women, who were now looking at Riya and Raghav, possibly wondering who Raghav was.

"I did meet some really relevant people. This was useful."

"That is great. Jaipur is after all, a huge hub for textiles and clothing. I wonder why you never explored this market."

They continued their discussion as they left the event venue. "So where are we going now?" asked Riya, as Raghav drove through the mild evening rush, which was new to the landscape of Jaipur, owing to the fast growing population and better business opportunities in the city.

He was driving his car in his city after long. He loved it. He loved the evening breeze of Jaipur, the splendid dusk visible in the backdrop of the majestic *Vidhan Sabha* building.

"For a quick drink somewhere, as you later have a dinner appointment at my home!"

"You sure, right? Meeting your parents, without any context. Isn't that weird?"

"What? My friends come to my place often. They have heard about you. Trust me; it is going to be normal."

They chatted as Raghav drove into a dark parking area. He escorted Riya to an archaic pub, dimly lit with beautiful sofa seating all around and a classy bar right in the centre. It was an extremely romantic setup, while the exalted and lofty Amer Fort of Jaipur in the background added to the overall charm, unique only to Jaipur.

Riya blushed, as they found a seat close to the bar and ordered for their first round of drinks.

Raghav bent a little and planted a romantic kiss on her cheek. She smiled at him and looked deep into his eyes.

"Riya, I don't have anything at the moment to promise you a rosy future or paint a picturesque life in front of you, with me."

"Raghav, you know…"

"No, let me speak. I want to tell you this. I have no idea of what I will be doing next. I think about it day and night, and of course, you know that. You go through and bear my conversations every day," said Raghav. Riya held his hand softly and looked at him.

"I have never been this free. I wake up in the morning with nothing to look forward to. I have lost the kick of meeting new people, networking, that vibe of taking the stage and the sheer intoxication of sales. I have no definitive future planned. I look for jobs most of the day on LinkedIn, and think about starting something new the rest of the time. I am nothing and I don't know how there will ever be a future for us in such a circumstance."

"Raghav…" Riya cleared her throat, still looking into his eyes and said, "I have seen you through this entire time. I have seen your ups as well. I have seen your capabilities and I believed in you, I fell in love with you. Whatever you do next, may it be a job or a venture, you will make yourself and everyone around you proud. And I want to be with you in making all of this again, in building things together."

"But, I have a dark past as well. You know a lot of it, but not all of it as yet."

"And a dark past only means a man with more stories to tell!"

Raghav laughed with a heavy throat. "You are too optimistic."

"Raghav, I just love you," said Riya, holding his hand stronger with conviction.

"And I love you too, more than I could have ever imagined at this stage of life!"

After another hour of intense conversation and dark humour that they exchanged, they finally drove to Raghav's place. Riya had emotions going through her mind like a mess. She was nervous about meeting his parents, but at the same time was trying to be casual about it, as it was a meeting like a friend.

The drive through Jaipur helped her ease out her mind. They crossed iconic buildings she had read about since childhood as tourist destinations. However, she did not feel like a tourist. She felt as if it was her own, as if she was never new here. Raghav's company and the weather made it a city of her own. Relatively smaller and growing cities have a charm of their own. They feel cosier, as if they are hugging you to be one of their own.

She entered his house with a mix of thrill and nervousness. They exchanged introductions as she looked around with interest.

"Mom, Dad… She is my close friend that I told you about – Riya."

With the first few awkward minutes of pleasantries, Raghav tried to break the ice by telling them about Riya and her work experience with different domains. He told them about her talk and they congratulated her for the great work.

By the time they moved to dinner, Riya had bypassed her initial nervousness and hesitation and talked to them about everything from work, weather to travel experiences, families and politics. When people in India discuss politics on a dinner table without heated arguments, you know things are going in the right direction. The conversations went on for a while even as the dinner finished and Raghav felt elated with how everything went. There was a sense of comfort and Raghav's parents engaged with Riya in a pleasant manner.

As they finished their dinner and Raghav helped his mother arrange the utensils back in the kitchen, his mother smiled and cheekily said, "So, Riya… your 'close' friend. How close is she?"

After all, she knew him better than anyone else in the world and there was no hiding possible. He simply smiled, gleefully ignoring her comment as he tried to hide the blush on his face. His mother stared at him, obviously intrigued with a child-like happiness on the face of a 28-year-old man.

He avoided the discussion and left with the excuse of dropping Riya to her hotel.

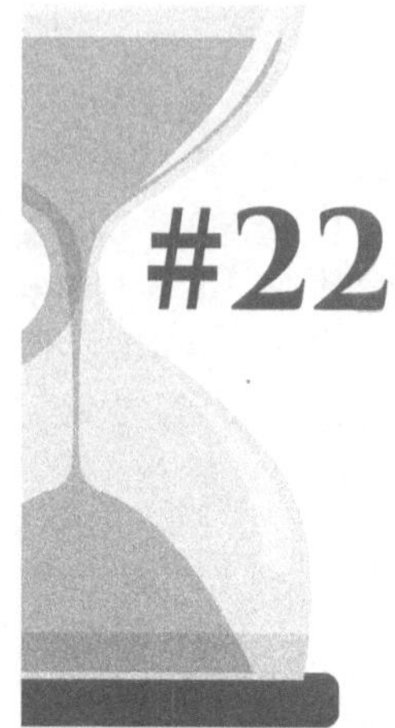

#22

Raghav sat in the outer area of his favourite tea cafe of the city—Chaisa was quietly nestled in one of the busiest locations of Jaipur—a beautiful cafe with both outdoor and indoor seating. Raghav had been an everyday visitor of this place for almost nine years now. He smoked a cigarette and tried to clear his thoughts in the cloud of smoke that he puffed out. Riya had gone back to New Delhi. The days spent with her were possibly the best days of Raghav's life so far. They had visited tourist destinations together, the most happening pubs of the city, enjoyed the nightlife of Jaipur, and driven through the calmest of roads for hours talking about what future awaits them.

Raghav scrolled through his messages on LinkedIn, as he stubbed his cigarette and sipped on his Masala Chai. After much deliberation and days of unending uncertainty and indecision, he had almost finalised on one job offer in New

Delhi for the time being. He had been offered the designation of VP-Business in one of the fastest growing data analysis companies of India. He had set his mind on this role and decided to go ahead with it until the time a business idea struck him, which he was no longer sure of conceiving. He had convinced himself that a job was the right thing to do at this stage of his career. Not only will this take his mind off the entire experience, but will also give him a new insight to the corporate world once again. He had not accepted the offer yet, and every day he thought of doing it by the end of the day. His procrastination was the result of overthinking and his debacle of having run something of his own for the last three years.

He often thought about his VigyaPun days and he could not bring himself to terms with what had happened. He had maturely accepted the reality, but a piece of his mind always kept going back to those days.

He had lost the mind space of entrepreneurship. It has to come to you naturally, which it did not. He sat there thinking about going back to a job and reporting to the founder of a company as an employee. Millions of people in the country work for someone else he often consoled himself. But was he really made for that?

"Tch Tch… the poster boy of Jaipur's startup ecosystem, sitting alone in Chaisa?"

Raghav turned around at the entry gate of the cafe to see who called him out. It was Yogesh, one of the investors of his company, who had actively seeked funds for them during the time of peril.

"Uh! Yogesh, how have you been?" said Raghav, shaking his hand, "Long time!"

"Indeed! You have almost been invisible since everything went awry," said Yogesh, as they stood in the aisle of tables amidst the greenery of plants in the outer area of Chaisa.

"I have just been trying to pull myself together," Raghav said in all honesty. "I have been looking up for jobs."

"Yeah! I think that is for the best. It is always at times like this, that one has to question if they ever even had an entrepreneurial streak," Yogesh said with an evil smile. The sarcasm in his voice was evident. Raghav had not expected him to put him down like this. Yogesh was one of the strongest supporters of the technology aspect of the product. He had put forward his opinion strongly about having come on board in the first place because there was technology involved. Otherwise, VigyaPun was just a content service company, in his words.

"Not just that, I wanted something for the time being to distract myself. I do not have a business idea to start right away."

"I suggest you don't, Raghav. As a well-wisher, I really believe you should straighten up your life now. Kumar and I were just talking the other day about you, out of genuine concern. At 28, you need to stop playing around for jest and start thinking of settling down."

"Thanks…"said Raghav, trying to match his sarcasm. "… For the concern!"

"Always, my boy!" Yogesh patted him on his arm. " I have

seen hundreds of entrepreneurs and meet a lot of them every day. I am a businessman myself. You know, some of us have it and some of us just don't. It is best that you look for a well-paying job for yourself, which shall not be difficult with your credentials, I am sure!"

"How is Pradeep Sir doing?" asked Raghav, trying to change the topic and end the conversation.

"He is fine. He has been off investing for a couple of weeks now. I guess he expected way too much out of VigyaPun. I always warned him not to trust a bunch of newbies. You understand Raghav, we as investors have to spread out our portfolio to be able to take a loss such as VigyaPun."

Raghav was hit hard. Not that he had ever minded anyone saying things, but this was at a time when he was already struggling and low. A part of him wanted to punch Yogesh, but the other part thought that maybe he was right. Maybe Raghav never had it in him. What he had seen in the last few months had mellowed him down and made him think. He kept quiet and smiled courteously through the rest of the conversation. Yogesh bragged about his portfolio companies and how a gaming company with Artificial Intelligence at its core, was on to raising another round of funds in tune of a million dollars. Raghav ignored all of it blatantly, trying to find an end to the conversation.

Thankfully, as soon as Yogesh walked away, Rahul stepped in. He looked at Raghav and immediately embraced him in a tight hug full of warmth and love. Rahul was the owner of the cafe, a humble entrepreneur who had started Chaisa out of his sheer love for tea and serving people with love. The smell of fresh tealeaves and the warmth of Rahul's welcoming smile were the only two things that made the cafe what it was.

Having been a regular visitor since the first day of the cafe, Raghav was like a younger brother to Rahul. Everyone in the city knew about their mutual love, given the cross promotion that they often did for each other on social media and through word of mouth. Rahul sat down as he lit a cigarette from Raghav's pack and ordered another round of tea on their table.

"I came to know about VigyaPun from the news. Is this what our relationship has come to?"

"Since when have you started following startup news platforms, in the first place?" Raghav said pleasantly surprised, pulling Rahul's leg.

"Someone shared it with me, as people know about our closeness! But that is not the bloody point," said Rahul and thumped the table. "You have been completely off the radar. No WhatsApp, no update on Facebook, you did not even tell me that you were moving back to Jaipur!"

"Uh! I haven't been in the mind space of talking to anyone. All of it just sucks."

"I understand. Of course it does. But you are responsible for this," said Rahul matter of factly. This was how their relationship had always been. Rahul was extremely straightforward, blunt and genuinely concerned about Raghav. He would never mince his words to something that he wanted to hear. And that is exactly why Raghav reciprocated the love. He respected

Rahul as an elder brother because he spoke the truth that was always needed to be heard.

Having people around you, who sugar coat their words, the so-called 'yes-men', are the worst kind of people.

"Uh? How?" said Raghav, unexpectedly taken aback by the directness of Rahul's statement.

"The first day when you started VigyaPun and came here late in the evening, we sat here while you furiously typed on your laptop. What was the idea back then, Raghav?"

"Umm…"

"No no, you answer me. What was your idea for which you gave up a well-paying job and your career as a consultant?" Rahul asked again, persistently looking for an answer from Raghav.

"To create good quality campaigns and content for every brand and business, big or small…" Raghav said softly, almost guilty as charged.

"And then you went to Delhi, raised funds and I don't know how it became a technology company doing data analysis and insights."

"That was the need of the market. That was where the money was…"

"Money! Ah!" said Rahul, banging his fist on the table. "Money always is where your heart is, Raghav. You wanted to woo some stupid investors, who think technology is a must to run a profitable business."

"But the unit economics…"

"Uh! Raghav, I am no 'startup guru'. I don't understand the terminology and the big words you all use. I am a small time businessman running this simple run of the mill cafe. You want to hear my cafe's 'differentiating factor' and how it is not a 'me-too'? Aren't these the words that your ecosystem uses? Tell me…" Rahul said, mocking the startup terminology

"Uh…" Raghav was at loss of words. Rahul was almost at the verge of scolding him. He was the first person in weeks who had genuinely not cared to satisfy Raghav's ego or motivate him in any way. He was the brother who said what needed to be spoken.

"So my 'USP' is bloody nothing. I serve tea with love. People love coming here because what I serve or the experience I create is more relatable to them and they love it. In nine years, I have only this one cafe that I have built with blood and sweat. And this is my business."

Raghav looked at him, believing in every word that he said.

"Raghav, sometimes business is all about keeping things simple. The simpler it is the more love it gets. This entire startup bubble has bloody lost the meaning of keeping things simple and creating a revenue generating business!"

"I guess you are right," said Raghav, introspecting. "I always knew I should have kept my original idea and not get swayed. We pivoted a lot and ultimately all of this happened. But now, there is no use crying over it. It just sucks…"

"Huh! Stop lamenting over it now. Anyway, I wanted to discuss this important thing with you," said Rahul, again switching the topic casually as if nothing had happened.

"Yes, tell me!" Raghav sighed out of relief of finally a change of topic. These days he just did not want to talk about startups and failures.

"So it is the 10-year anniversary of the cafe in three months. We are completely revamping it. I am getting the interiors redone, the colours, the walls, the menus; simply everything will be turned around. It has been ten years of the same old stuff and now it's time to bring a whole new Chaisa to people."

"That sounds great!" Raghav said excitedly. He felt amazing that the cafe that had been a part of his growing up in the city was now a decade old. He had flashbacks of all those memories and moments that he had spent here. "How can I be of any help?"

"Yeah! So, I want the entire campaign done by you. Whatever you say! The content planning, the ads that go out, social media campaigns, radio, print, the content and the kind of designs that go up in the interiors, the quirk element in the menu – everything!"

Raghav was silent for a few seconds as Rahul looked at him anticipating a reaction.

"Rahul, I don't know! You don't have to pity, bro…"

"Fuck you! Will you get out of your mourning for your closed 'tech-startup'?" said Rahul laughing at him. "You remember those couplets you wrote on tea for us six years ago?"

"Yeah, I do..."

"And you know how that went, right? Marketing websites and ad news portals featured us. It went viral. Everyone in Jaipur knew us after that. People re-shared it like crazy. You know why?"

"Why?" Raghav asked innocently, trying to keep up with the pace and excitement of Rahul.

"Because you wrote it from your heart. You kept it 'simple'. People could relate with it. And that is exactly what I need. I need someone who has their heart in Chaisa, who has seen it grow. I need your words, Raghav. I need your ideas and your thoughts. And you know you are good at it, which is why you made this your business in the first place!" Rahul sounded convincing.

"Yes, but that was not my business for a majority of the last three years. I was into developing tech, testing softwares we developed, analysing marketing data, predicting trends with artificial intelligence..."

"Fuck all of that tech gyaan. I need the heart that you had for content and campaigns."

"And what about the design? You know I have an eye for it, but I don't design myself."

"That is like my boy, finally thinking!" said Rahul, slapping him on his back. "I know Disha is back in town as well."

Disha and Raghav had spent a lot of time in the initial months of VigyaPun at Chaisa, ideating, executing and developing business. Disha had a good rapport with Rahul, considering that he had a knack of treating everyone with a welcoming smile and love.

"Rahul, I just had to let go of the entire team. We don't work together any more. Moreover, I have been out of touch with everyone for the last one month. She might have started working somewhere now!"

"At least talk to her, otherwise we will figure something out," said Rahul trying to get Raghav to agree. He winked and said, "I will even pay!"

"Fuck you! The day I have to take money for what I write for Chaisa, is the day I will stop writing!" said Raghav with a smile, lighting another cigarette. "I will do it, you know that already!"

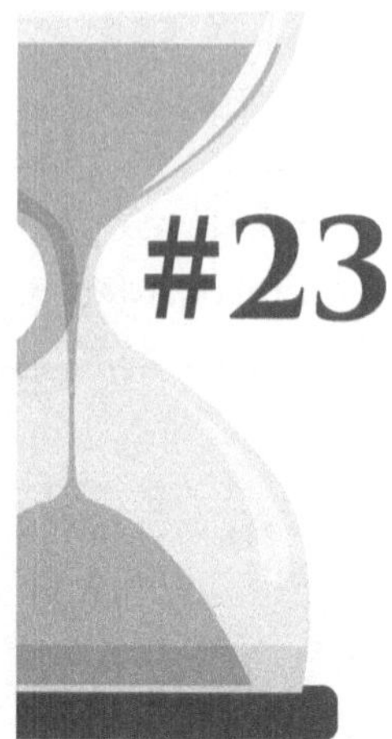

#23

Hung up on the future,
He often lived in the past
He let the present go by,
So void, so vast

Raghav woke up gasping for breath. He was sweating as he drank half a bottle of water to regain his senses. He checked the time. It was already seven in the morning. Dreams had been troubling him for some time now. *"You need to stop playing around for jest and start thinking of settling down."* Yogesh's words had been screaming in his dream before he woke up, almost jostled.

His nights were often troubled even now. He remained awake most of his nights thinking about the past and worried about his future. Sudden thoughts like accepting the offer of his new job often made him uncomfortably shift in his bed for hours. Sometimes, he just felt sweaty and pukish just by thinking about why he started up in the first place, leaving his consulting career.

He woke up and forced himself out of the bed. The whiff of

breakfast filled his nostrils, as he knew it was breakfast time at his house already. Without a second thought and completely ignoring the fact that they did not work together any more, he dialled Disha's number right away.

"All good with you, Rathore?" Raghav asked Disha, as he called her at a time that was not even civil enough. He often addressed her by her surname, as it denoted a suave Rajput tradition that came along with it.

"You are alive!" Disha sarcastically exclaimed, still sounding sleepy.

"Thankfully! You managed to get a job for yourself?" Raghav asked rather insensitively.

"No. Did not look for anything actively so far. I have not been able to overcome what we went through. But why?"

"Meet at 11? Chaisa?" said Raghav, asserting their personal equation.

"Uh! Why do I always listen to you! Of course!" said Disha and hung up.

Raghav explained to her the entire project in the exact words that Rahul had used. He tried to imitate the same excitement and exuberance as well. As he specifically wrote down all the deliverable points Rahul had mentioned on a tissue paper and Disha in her utter disbelief asked questions, they sipped countless cups of tea.

"Any question?" asked Raghav, as he wrapped up his discussion with timelines that he had thought. He wanted to convince Disha as he had been pulled into it. For Raghav, this was more of a distraction from the hollowness and emptiness building inside him. He hoped for his dreams to be replaced with content and stories.

"Yes. Why do you want me to do this? And moreover, why are you doing this in the first place?"

"Disha, look at this," he said pointing at the entire discussion on the tissue paper. "This is what we had always wanted to do. And this is just a one-off opportunity for me to just feel closer to content building and storytelling that I have always loved. I know this doesn't pay, nor does it come with any future. To be very honest with you, this is a heartfelt attempt by me to feel closer to my home in more ways than one."

"Raghav, I understand. But this is a delusion, a diversion. What is your plan? I have already applied for a couple of jobs and I am expecting to join somewhere in Jaipur in a month or less. But I am worried about you."

"I have been looking at jobs as well. I have an offer waiting for my acceptance in Delhi. We will be fine. We will move on, get settled in our jobs and never look back again. Who knows, we might not even have time to stay in touch with each other, for God's sake! We will be busy. We are fast moving, young millennials, and you know we will be engrossed in our own lives once we get back to working," Raghav said animatedly. He meant every word of what he said.

"You have a month, right? Let us work together for one last time, just for fun. No pressure of deadlines, no client meetings, no financial troubles. Let us give a shot to what we were always good at."

"Uh... I can't turn you down, ever," said Disha, with scepticism in herself.

"So, we are on, eh Rathore?" said Raghav and high-fived her.

For the next couple of days, they sat together at Chaisa brainstorming about content ideas, design thoughts, and how they could bring out the homelike and close-to-heart emotion through words and colours. The entire idea was to re-create the feeling of comfort to make the regular clients relate to the cafe and create a recall in the mind of the clients that they know this place. Nevertheless, tea was the most important binding element across everything. Two things that always bound people together were tea and cigarettes! Nothing like a good smoke along with a cup of tea to start a conversation.

They studied every minute detail about the cafe, which they had never noticed in so many years. Raghav excitedly spoke to Riya about everything they did, every night. She loved listening to his ideas and his vision of re-branding his favourite cafe. She shared his exhilaration, as she loved seeing him all worked up about ideas again.

"We need a better place to work, Raghav and specially, to now execute all these ideas," Disha said mockingly showing him all the tissue papers that were filled with text and graphs and designs. "I need my software now and a high speed internet."

"Umm. You are right. Our productivity will be slower until the time we work from Chaisa. Plus the millions of people, who walk in and out, wave, greet and meet us. Even in all these years, Jaipur has remained the same. Everyone knows everyone," said Raghav, in a warm way rather than sounding complaining at all.

"We can't even work from home. We need to sit together to bring out these ideas. Anyway your eccentricities bring out a new idea of content every minute that we sit together and I need to cope up with those at a faster pace, with a faster internet."

"We could work from my home…" Raghav was thinking out loud. "But again, there are a hundred other things that parents keep on bringing up when they see you at home."

Disha nodded in agreement. She looked at Raghav and almost in a whisper asked, "Is 426, SBS Tower not available anymore?"

She was referring to their Jaipur office of VigyaPun. It was also the first office where they had started the company from. Raghav did not react weirdly. Wrapping up his tissue papers together, he said, "Uh, it is. It is anyway my dad's owned property. I could use it for a couple of days for this."

They drove to SBS Tower in C-Scheme, the business hub of Jaipur. It was a four storeyed massive building and their humble office had been on the top floor. As Raghav unlocked the door, a strong smell of untouched papers and dust filled their senses. It had been closed for more than a month. A 200 square feet small room only had a long table in the centre with chairs all around and few beanbags kept in the far corner. To the extreme right of the entry door there was a small table for water, tiffins, electric kettle for tea or coffee. The opposite end had a small washroom. Disha and Raghav looked at each other. Both were lost in the conundrum of time and memories.

This was the office where Disha had given her interview to Raghav. This is where they had acquired their first client and the white board on the wall, where they brainstormed all their ideas. This is where Raghav had dreamed of creating the biggest content and marketing consulting company of India and shared his vision with the rest of the team members with passion. This is where all the first announcements had come – raising funds, opening a Delhi office, reaching the first milestone of revenues.

Raghav suddenly realised the decision of coming back to this office was not after all, the best decision. This office had been a happy space full of people with parties, drinks, laughter, celebrations and emotions.

Raghav called the building cleaner and he arrived in less than five minutes greeting Raghav. He started cleaning the entire office. Raghav waited outside. The corridor ended in a small balcony next to the elevator. He smoked and watched intently down on the busy road.

"You okay?" asked Disha.

"Uh, yes! All of this got over sooner than I had thought."

"You had thought of it? I had never even imagined. I always thought working for VigyaPun, working on creative ideas was my calling for a lifetime!" said Disha almost close to tears.

"You will find a job suitable for your calibre," said Raghav almost consoling her.

"Ha!" she laughed sarcastically. "I will never be able to work on something like my own."

"Neither of us will…" said Raghav thinking about the job he had finalised for himself. He had given up on the idea of entrepreneurship, as he had no confidence on whether he would ever be able to sell anything for himself again.

They entered the office, took a beanbag each and started working away on their laptops.

The next few days passed by in a jiffy. Raghav realised how he had started thinking about the project so deeply and about the endless loop of his past and the future less. He used to wake up through the nights again, but this time passionately coming up with ideas to make the campaign of re-branding Chaisa a success.

It was a lot more than just his relationship with Rahul now. It was about proving to people that he still had it in him. He drowned himself in work with a weird aggression. Almost after two months, he was working so deeply on something. The last few months had flown by before his eyes, working on the legalities of shutting down a company and helping his team members be placed.

Raghav and Disha remembered their time in the office quite often. They had the same kind of fun again working together. They had decided to make the most out of the last month of working together.

"So, we have almost designed the whole campaign. The only thing remaining now is planning the rollout and closing in on partnerships and media buying. By the way, we are also meeting Rahul this weekend to show him what we have done," Raghav announced to Disha, as they had spent three weeks working on the project day and night. They had to plan for five months of campaign and marketing. Without the support of a full-fledged team, they had to do everything on the project themselves. Their project was almost at a close now.

"Uh, that is great!" said Disha, clapping her hands together. "And then, we are done! All of this will finally be over..." She said going in a stream of thoughts looking around at the office.

"Indeed!" said Raghav, with a sad smile.

Raghav's phone rang as he walked out of the office in the corridor to attend the call. "Hey! We were just talking about our meeting."

"Of course, we are on for Saturday afternoon, right?" asked Rahul, confirming again.

"Yes. We are all set. Tell me, why did you ring up?"

"Uh, yeah! So actually, I have two more friends who want to rebrand their businesses as well, coincidentally. One of them..."

"Uh, Rahul...wait! I told you it would just be for you. I am not doing this professionally. And you know I have a job to join in less than a month now. Disha has to join in around a week. I told you clearly!"

"I know! I told them the same. But everyone knows you, they have seen you work. Now that they know you are back in town, they want to work with you and are ready to pay anything you ask!"

"Rahul, I don't have..." Raghav was short of words. He did not know what to say. After a small argument, he hung up. He tried convincing Rahul how he had decided to settle down in a job. Doing this again and going through the entire pain was something he dreaded from the bottom of his heart. Rahul, however, was convinced that Raghav had it in him. He told him repeatedly on how it was the wrong decision of letting multiple people meddle in his business vision. Rahul had a point. Raghav loved doing this. Together with his team, he created stuff that clients loved. His vision had always been clear, until the time he was pushed into the startup current and lost his originality, to become one of the thousands of Tech-startups.

Lost deep in his thoughts, he entered the office and drank a bottle of water. He was thinking something hard, Disha could make out. He walked to the white board and with a red marker wrote on the top in massive size '2.0.'

"What?" asked Disha, still confused and worried about Raghav. She often thought he would go mad. She knew how messed up a place his brain was. She knew Raghav could not sit still for more than a few minutes without creativity and ideas flowing inside him. He underlined the words written on the board and exclaimed, "Why don't we do this for a living? This is what we always envisioned on doing. Let us do it professionally for a living!"

#24

Raghav was not sure about Disha's response, if she would be willing to take another chance in a new venture. After all, working with a startup at this stage is a huge risk for one's career. Contrary to what he had expected, Disha agreed immediately, which in itself was a huge testimony of her belief in Raghav's leadership capabilities. Things like this had humbled Raghav over the past few months.

Riya was enthusiastic too. She was the first person Raghav called when Disha and he had worked out the specifics.

"So the idea is to create content-led marketing campaigns and do some real creative shit!" Raghav told Riya with excitement, which was almost on the verge of delirium. Raghav was short of breath. It was an awkward situation. He had always known he wanted to do this, but he was swayed. It was more like a homecoming, rather than starting something new. Somehow, he just needed that little push over the edge, to visit his vision again and believe in what he did best.

"There has never been better news for me, Raghav."

"Riya, I love you for having stuck with me through this. No technology, no funding, no shenanigans. We might not have a USP or a differentiating factor. But… uh, but we have a heart in our business and we are doing to create stuff that people love! We are going to be a real business!"

"I love that part. I love hearing about it. You know what, just get back to it and tell me about it later at night!" said Riya and encouraged him to focus on more specifics and thrashing the idea in and out. She knew he needed time. She felt a streak of happiness beyond words.

"Of course! Riya, I cannot wait to see you and be with you. I have found it. This is what I always wanted to do. The sheer kick that I got from creating this entire campaign was what I was looking for since two years now."

"Raghav, welcome back to being the entrepreneur that you are. Kill it!"

He went back inside the office elated. By this time, Disha had drawn up a three-months planning chart for their three clients now. In the next few days, Raghav updated his LinkedIn, had a new website created and the legalities of a simple partnership firm done for the time being. He completed all the hygiene involved in getting this off the ground.

They shared a campaign profile of the work they did on social media and the reviews raved about it. Raghav's LinkedIn was alive with love and appreciation, and he finally turned down the job offer politely. Few more sales conversations were initiated in the next few days as Disha worked out the operational bit of it with three new interns. They decided to target the brands and businesses of Jaipur first, with the simple policy of not saying No to anyone – big or small.

They had to keep it lean and increase the profitability this time around, having learned from their experiences in the past.

Raghav could finally make some sense of his life. He remembered his moment in Varanasi, the words of his father that he would always have his back, his conversation with Yogesh outside Chaisa and finally how Rahul gave him the golden advice of 'keeping it simple'. He was back to running a business, and ironically, from where his entrepreneurial career started – his first office. He did things his way, led by example, and kept his team motivated with his previously popular weekend parties. It was all there again, all created by him – and this time, with a whole new experience.

A few months later, he received a call from an unknown number in their newly but minimalistically furnished office, which Disha felt was important for a fresh start and new perspectives. Hoping for a new sales lead, Raghav picked up the phone and answered soberly.

"Hello, this is Raghav."

"Raghav, this is Shashank Bhardwaj from Mumbai. You might have heard of me or my company The Vision 200."

Raghav could slightly recall something from his startup network. Shashank, without waiting for a response continued, "I went through your profile and saw your work with your new company. It is impressive and I was wondering if you wanted to apply for our upcoming pitch day. We are committing a fund of $1 Million to the winning startup."

Suddenly, a full vision of startup events, pitching, presentations, negotiation, and term sheets filled Raghav's mind and without another second of delay, he responded, "Thanks a lot for the offer Shashank. But we are not looking to raise... ever."

He smiled to himself and hung up, walking back into his office with a new found entrepreneurial streak and a confidence that came from failures.

Disha looked at him smiling and said, "You have done all of this before. You know how it's done. But yet, you are gleeful like a child!"

"Entrepreneurship is the best roller coaster that the world could offer. It is always 'The First Time', Disha... Always 'The First Time'!"

9 789390 463923